Granada, Surrender!

CARL KIDWELL

THE VIKING PRESS

NEW YORK

To Tresa, Marie, Anna, Joe

Contents

Mountain Foray

In the dawn's first light the city was only a shadowy mass, looming on the skirts of the mountains a few miles away. But Pedro knew that turbaned heads lined every battlement and tower, that black eyes were blazing hatred as they looked down at the encampment in the plain. A prickle ran along his spine. It wasn't fear—at least he hoped it wasn't—but just an awareness of danger, and the suspense of uncertainty. The men around him felt it too. It was plain in every face— except Chico's.

Not even a hostile Moorish city could bother Chico, Pedro thought, looking down at the young soldier beside him. He had to look well down, for though Pedro was no taller than average for his fifteen years, he topped Chico by a full head. Chico's round face looked quite untroubled, as expressionless as the moon. His placid appearance had a steadying effect, and Pedro's uneasiness subsided.

"Ay, Chico! Is there no end to marching?" Pedro fetched a mock groan. "We just got here yesterday. Now we're off again."

"What matter? We'll be back in a few days." Chico's voice was as placid as his face.

"Yes, but who knows what we'll miss while we're gone?

Suppose action should break out here, while we're out foraging in the mountains. Why, maybe the Moors are getting set
for battle right this minute."

Chico shrugged, unconcerned. "Maybe. Maybe not."

Pedro wondered what might be going on in the mind behind that serene face. Odd, he reflected, that although he
and Chico were the best of friends, they weren't at all well
acquainted. Chance had thrown them together the week
before, when the army mustered to begin the spring campaign. Near the same age, and both new to military life, they
had naturally sought each other's company. But, as Pedro
was fast learning, they made oddly matched friends—he with
his high-strung temperament and Chico with his stolid, never-
ruffled calm.

Pedro gave up trying to read the other's mind and looked
with still fresh interest at his surroundings. To think that
only yesterday this place had been as empty as a desert! The
camp had sprung up as if by a sorcerer's command—a vast
expanse of tented canvas, vividly colored, set amid a forest of
fluttering pennons. It was still unfinished. More tents were
going up even now, early as it was, and countless soldiers,
busy at countless tasks, milled about among the heaps of
supplies and equipment that cluttered the area. At the
camp's edge a battle-ready unit stood guard, alert for any sign
of enemy action.

"Leave all excess gear in camp, men—we'll travel light."
An officer bawled the order—quite unnecessarily, Pedro
thought, for the troops had already received their instructions. The man added a grim pleasantry. "Don't forget your
weapons—it's hostile country in those mountains."

Pedro tightened his grip on his pike, feeling a little thrill of eagerness—or maybe it was apprehension. He turned back to Chico.

"You know, Chico, maybe we're lucky at that, being assigned to this detachment. We may see more excitement than these fellows who stay here in camp."

A blare of trumpets drowned out Chico's reply. Shouts and orders sounded, laggards came scurrying, there was a brief scramble as soldiers fell into formation, and captains spurred to the heads of their units.

"All units, *for-r-r-ward!*"

Like a steel-spiked river, the columns moved out across the plain. Hoofbeats and marching feet drummed like muted thunder, raising clouds of red dust that hung over the marchers in drifts. The sun's first rays, slanting over the horizon, filtered through the haze and struck cold fire from arms and armor. It was a sight to stir any man's blood, especially that of an eager young man like Pedro. With a sense of wonder, still strong after days on the march, he squinted against the dust and peered at the long columns that stretched ahead.

This detachment was no mere foraging party—it was a formidable force, prepared to cope with any opposition it might encounter. The forward divisions were made up of light-armored cavalry and platoons of crossbowmen and arquebusiers. Crack troops they were, splendidly accoutered, a dazzling array of color and luster.

The common soldiers who followed looked drab by comparison. There were some seasoned troops among them, but many were farmers, tradesmen, craftsmen, or laborers, turned

soldiers only for the duration of this campaign. Nearly all
wore their own civilian clothes, though here and there a helmet or cuirass gave a military touch. Their ragged formation
looked anything but military, but Pedro felt very soldierly indeed as he marched with them, his pike slanted smartly
across his shoulder.

In the rear came a large train of pack animals, some carrying the provisions needed for the march, others unburdened,
ready to be loaded with the supplies the troops would doubtless capture.

The columns headed toward a point well to the right of
the city. Eagerly Pedro scanned the mountain range ahead.
Hostile country, the officer had said. It didn't look hostile.
While rugged and awesome, it was also beautiful, the lower
slopes a tawny-gold in the sun and the summits glistening
with snow. Impulsively, he touched Chico's arm.

"Look, Chico—those mountains! All bright and brown,
with the peaks so shiny-white. They look like—like gold
and silver."

Chico considered the comparison doubtfully. "They look
like mountains to me," he said matter-of-factly.

Pedro gave a little sigh, then a little grin. Figures of speech
were lost on the literal-minded Chico. He turned from his
short comrade to the man at his other side, a friendly remark
on the tip of his tongue. But the man's forbidding aspect
made him bite off the words. Pedro gathered a swift impression of a massive build, a bristling beard and a scarred, fierce-
looking face, hard and weathered as a mountain boulder.

Again his eyes turned toward the city, and a sudden sense
of strangeness gripped him. Even now it was hard to realize

that he was actually a soldier, taking part in military operations in the very shadow of Granada.

Granada! To Pedro—to all of Spain—the name held both magic and menace. For centuries the city had been the pride of the Moors, the heart of the Moslem kingdom that bordered Christian Spain. But the Spanish armies in recent years had pushed their way into that kingdom, taking city after city until now only Granada remained, the last stronghold of Moslem power.

The city shimmered like a mirage in the dust-dimmed sunlight. It looked impregnable, half surrounded as it was by rugged mountains and barricaded by miles of massive walls. But could mountains and walls and human courage withstand the might of Spain?

Pedro heard the thought echoed in the talk around him.

"I'll stake gold against copper that Boabdil surrenders the city without a fight."

"Don't count on that. Even a coward will fight when he's cornered—and Boabdil is no coward."

"He's no fool, either. His army is no match for ours, and he knows it. Just wait until our cannons start battering those walls—he'll surrender fast enough."

Pedro had heard that same talk ever since the army started its march to Granada. Who could know what Boabdil would do? Probably the Moorish ruler himself didn't know.

Again he spoke to Chico, his eyes still on the city. "Those walls look strong enough to stand against anything, even cannons."

A response came, but not from Chico. Pedro gave a little start as the fierce-faced man spoke.

"We'll not use cannons." His voice boomed like a deep-toned bell, making Pedro's eardrums ring. The man looked at him, and Pedro felt himself shriveling under the fierce stare, like a leaf under a burning glass. "The King wants Granada in one piece, not in a heap of rubble. We won't attack the city—we'll besiege it. I'd stake a golden dobla on that, if I had one. Since I haven't, I'll stake my reputation—and believe me, youngster, that isn't much to risk." With startling suddenness, his face softened into a smile.

Pedro returned the smile a bit uncertainly. He didn't know this bearded giant, though he'd seen him among the troops several times. He'd heard him, too—that booming voice could carry through half the army. The man's smile faded, leaving his face fierce again, but a friendly glint still lingered in his eyes.

"Your first taste of soldiering, I take it?"

Pedro was disconcerted by the question. He had fondly imagined that after a whole week in the army he might pass for a seasoned veteran. "That's right, sir," he said.

The "sir" came quite naturally—Pedro had been taught always to address his elders with respect—but it seemed to annoy the man. "Oh, come now, youngster, don't 'sir' me—I'm not a grandee. Marcos is my name—Marcos Olmedo." He looked questioningly at Pedro, who responded quickly.

"My name is Pedro. Pedro Tegero." This time he left off the "sir."

Marcos's glance flicked toward Pedro's red stocking-cap, which smacked of the sea like a salt-laden breeze. "You're from some seaport, I'll wager."

"You're almost right," Pedro conceded. "I lived quite close to a port. At La Rábida."

"La Rábida? Just what and where might that be?"

Pedro shot him a surprised glance. He had assumed that the Monastery of Santa María de La Rábida was known throughout Christendom. "It's a monastery. Not far from Palos. You've never heard of it?"

"To tell the truth, Pedro, I'm not well informed about monasteries. I'm much better acquainted with taverns." Marcos chuckled slyly. "But what the devil were you doing in a monastery? Planning to become a monk?"

"*Vaya*, no! I'm an orphan, and I've lived at La Rábida for as long as I can remember. The friars there take care of homeless boys."

"I see." The man's glance slid past Pedro and rested on Chico, whose dark hose and plain rustic tunic were set off by a bright-green kerchief knotted around his head. "By your clothes, youngster, I'd guess you come from farther inland than Pedro here."

"Yes. My home is on a farm near Carmona." Chico paused, then evidently felt that more information was called for. "My name is Roberto Morales, but everybody calls me Chico."

Pedro's lips quirked. As if anyone as short as Chico could possibly be called anything else!

Marcos's stony face cracked into another smile. "One from a monastery, one from a farm. And now you're both soldiers! Me, now, I've been carrying arms so long I can hardly remember ever doing anything else." There was pride in the statement. "I've fought the Moors in every campaign since they took Zahara, back in 1481. Ten years ago, that was."

Pedro nodded, agreeing with the arithmetic but somewhat vague about the capture of Zahara. After all, he'd been only five when that happened.

"Ten years, ten campaigns," said Marcos. "And every one left me with another scar. Scars all over me, lads, though this is the only one that shows." His huge fingers stroked the long white mark on his cheek. "Got this in the siege of Baza, year before last. A scimitar grazed my cheek—*diablos!* if I hadn't ducked just in time it would've sliced off my head. But I've kept the score even—there's many a Moor carrying the mark of my blade on his heathen hide."

Pedro studied the man furtively, noting his much-nicked helmet and the crudely-mended cuts in his leather jerkin. Marcos was obviously a veteran campaigner. The scar, the beard, and the rugged features made his age hard to guess— thirty, thirty-five, perhaps even forty, Pedro thought. His build had the same mountain-boulder quality as his face— solid, massive, and roughly formed. Marching next to him, Pedro felt positively puny.

Marcos knew something of the region ahead, for the army had been here before. "We pushed well into the mountains when we were here last autumn," he told the two youths. "It's rugged country, but there are some real garden-spots tucked away in those hills—valleys as green and fertile as this vega used to be." His arm swept out to indicate the plain around them.

Pedro frowned slightly as his eyes followed the gesture. This Vega of Granada was normally farmland, as fertile, so he'd heard, as any in Spain. Now the once-green plain was a blackened desert. The army had swept into the vega the previous autumn, just before disbanding for the winter, destroying crops and burning farms in order to cut off the enemy's food supply.

"You youngsters missed that raid," Marcos went on. "*Diablos!* We didn't leave a green sprig standing. Now the turbaned devils have just two choices—surrender or starve." He fell silent for a moment, turning a thoughtful gaze toward the city. "You know, it's just possible that they'll choose to starve."

The troops were moving at a steady, mile-eating pace, skirting the city widely as they neared the borders of the mountain country. Behind them the camp lay like a colorful mosaic, hazed by dust and distance. Around them the vega baked in the sun, for its irrigation channels were dry and unused now. The only greenery was narrow bands of vegetation along the banks of streams. At intervals they passed abandoned hamlets and farmhouses, the clay-brick dwellings looking pathetic and lonely amid the ruins of orchards and gardens.

The army's earlier ravages remained evident even after the marchers left the vega and entered the lower reaches of the mountains. Both city and camp were soon lost to sight, hidden by intervening hills. Threading through demolished olive groves and stands of cork oak, they emerged upon a barren ridge, beyond which the going grew steadily rougher. All around were rolling hills, broken here and there by an abrupt precipice or a towering mass of bald rock. Icy streams, fed by the melting snow on the heights, leaped and tumbled through rocky gorges. Looking up, Pedro saw an eagle gliding in great circles far overhead. Lowering his eyes, he glimpsed a lizard darting across a rock like a streak of green flame.

Soaring eagles and earthbound lizards, but no people. The marchers had seen no one since they left the camp.

As they moved deeper into the mountains, contingents under separate commands were detached from the main force, ranging out in broad swathes to scour the region. Guides who knew the country accompanied each contingent, and scouts rode ahead as they advanced, alert for danger. Pedro's heart was beating in double time as he marched off with one of the contingents. He felt a twinge of uneasiness at the thought that the enemy city was much closer than the camp. Then his misgivings faded as he glanced down at Chico's placid face.

"Tired, Chico?" he asked.

Chico seemed surprised at the question. He shook his head decidedly. "No. Are you?"

Pedro nodded, just as decidedly. "Yes."

He needn't worry about Chico, he thought with an inner smile. Chico's legs were short, but they stretched into tireless strides.

The company was coming into territory not reached by earlier raids. The terrain gradually became less wild; steep cliffs began to merge into gentler slopes, and presently the marchers topped a brush-grown rise to see a broad cultivated valley opening up ahead. The hillsides were terraced for irrigation and planted with olive groves and vineyards, with grainfields and gardens on the lower inclines. On the slope that dropped away at their feet was a huddle of flat-roofed houses, looking like boxes piled one above another. There was no sign of life, and as the troops plunged down the hill they found the village deserted. The inhabitants, forewarned, had fled to the city with their flocks and what effects they could carry.

"To work, men!" came a shouted order. "See if they've left any provisions we can use. Destroy everything else."

What followed revolted Pedro. The houses were looted, the gardens trampled. Battle-axes demolished vineyards and hacked down blossoming orchards. The soldiers set fire to everything that would burn; everything else was wrecked. Pedro did what he had to, though it outraged the ideals he had absorbed at the monastery. It was the wantonness of the destruction that appalled him, the men's avid relish for their task. There were gleeful shouts; he saw warm, friendly faces suddenly become brutish. The sight increased his revulsion.

When the ravages were completed, the men gathered beside a stream just below the village, to rest and eat on its tree-shaded bank. Pedro ate in silence, ignoring the talk and laughter around him. Moodily he gazed at the smoking wreckage, at the hacked and trampled remains of green growing things. The hamlet's boxlike structures were gutted shells, their tiny windows staring like empty eyes at the ruin around them.

Pedro sighed heavily. This expedition wasn't turning out at all as he'd anticipated. He'd been eager for excitement. He hadn't bargained for anything like this—cruel and ugly and destructive. He looked at Chico, wondering if he too was bothered by such qualms. Apparently not. Chico was placidly munching his cheese and barley bread, seeming not at all disturbed at having just demolished someone's lovingly tended gardens.

Presently Pedro ventured a troubled remark. "It isn't pleasant, ruining people's farms—even if they *are* Moors."

Chico considered briefly, then gave his characteristic shrug. "If we ruin their crops, they don't eat. And if they don't eat, they can't fight."

"I know."

It was true, of course. The quickest way to end this war was to destroy the farms which supplied Granada with food. But, Pedro thought, destroying the enemy's food supply was one thing—wanton devastation was quite another. Frowning, he unfastened his leather flask from his belt, dashed out the stale water, and filled it afresh from the stream. A long drink made him feel better, and his frown smoothed out. He was a soldier, he reminded himself. And being a soldier was highly exciting, even if there were some very unpleasant duties involved.

A shouted order brought the men to their feet. Marcos, who had left the two youths when the ravages began, again fell in beside them. Pedro was pleased, though somewhat surprised that the seasoned veteran should seek the company of two raw recruits. He suspected that Marcos liked to talk of his colorful experiences, and enjoyed impressing the two young novices.

Pedro threw a last somber look at the ruin behind them. "Those villagers must have got away just before we came." He shook his head, puzzled. "Here we are, miles deep in enemy territory, and we haven't seen a single Moor."

"Do you expect them to stay home to welcome us?" Marcos asked dryly. "The warning has gone ahead that we're coming, you can count on that. By now the mountain people are swarming into Granada from miles around. *Diablos!* The city's going to be so packed they'll be bursting out the walls."

The big man's booming comments continued to batter Pedro's ears as the troops crossed the valley, forded a stream overhung with tamarisks, and swarmed up the farther slope. When they reached the crest, Marcos pointed to a smudge of smoke rising beyond a neighboring hill.

"The other contingents are busy with their torches too," he observed.

There was satisfaction in his tone, but Pedro felt another surge of revulsion. Was this what war was like? He'd always pictured it as something exciting, with army clashing against army, sword against scimitar. This sort of thing—ravaging homes and driving away families—hadn't even entered his imagination. He was glad when the valley dropped out of sight beyond the top of the rise.

Abruptly, the surroundings became rugged and barren, and soon the marchers again found themselves in a rocky wilderness where scarcely a green thing grew. It was a country of sudden contrasts—and sudden surprises.

The attack came swiftly, unexpectedly. Scouts, ranging out ahead, had seen nothing to indicate danger. But danger could be easily overlooked among these jutting spurs and brush-grown ravines. One minute there were only the sounds of casual talk, of footfalls and hoofbeats, of clinking harness and accouterments. The next, like deadly shafts of lightning, a volley of crossbow bolts hurtled into the column.

From a nearby ridge burst the blood-chilling war cry of the Moors.

"Allah-h akbar-r-r!"

From
Vandal to Herdsboy

For an instant Pedro went rigid, frozen between strides. A party of turbaned horsemen had crested the ridge. Their war cry echoed back and forth among the hills, as if countless voices were repeating the savage challenge from every direction. Then, before the startled marchers could so much as raise their weapons, the attackers whirled their mounts and vanished like phantoms over the rim of the ridge.

"*After them, men!*"

The soldiers snapped into action and surged up the slope. The Spanish battle cry rose in a mighty shout.

"*Santia-a-a-go!*"

Pedro's heart was thumping his ribs as he dashed up the incline. He was thoroughly excited, thoroughly scared. But his chief emotion was sheer amazement—he, Pedro Tegero, who never in his life had used anything more lethal than a garden hoe, was wielding a pike and pursuing a party of hostile Moors!

However, the pursuit was short. When the troops reached the crest, the only sign of the Moors was a flurry of red dust beyond the next ridge. The horsemen had evidently approached with weapons readied, and fled after a single volley,

without dismounting to rewind their crossbows. The Spaniards scowled at the dust cloud in frustration. There was no
thought of giving chase. Spanish horsemen in cumbersome
armor were no match for Moors on agile mounts, especially
in this tumbled terrain, the Moors' very element. The troops
milled about uncertainly for a few minutes, then retraced
their steps and began attending to the wounded.

There were only a few injuries, most of them minor, for
the Moors had been barely within range. The cavalrymen
had suffered worst. Two or three foot soldiers had taken light
injuries, and one was badly hurt, his leg pierced by a crossbow bolt. His comrades bandaged the wound with wine-
soaked cloths and placed him on one of the pack mules.
Then the march resumed, with alertness sharpened.

Pedro looked at the wounded men with commiseration.
Still shaky with excitement, he was surprised at how casually
the seasoned soldiers treated the episode.

"We can expect that sort of thing," Marcos said. "Boabdil is sending out parties of cavalry to put on some show of
resistance. They'll harass us like flies, but they can't do more
than slow us up."

"Why doesn't he send out his whole army?" Pedro
asked.

"And leave the city unguarded? He wouldn't dare—not
with *our* army camped right at his front door."

Chico made a completely irrelevant observation. "Some of
those Moors really had fine-looking horses."

Pedro threw him a look that was half amused, half
astonished. The sudden violence hadn't made a ripple in
Chico's calm. Imagine noticing horses at a time like that!

As Marcos predicted, the Moors seemed bent on harassing the advance rather than vainly trying to halt it. Their next thrust followed the same pattern as the first—a lightning assault and a swift withdrawal. But this time Spanish crossbows and arquebuses were ready, and some of the assailants were lolling in the saddle as they retreated.

Marcos peered after them sharply. "Those aren't trained troopers—not all of them, anyway. Look at their clothes, and their weapons. Some are only armed with spears. Citizens, I'll wager, pressed into emergency service. *Diablos!* No wonder they can't do us any damage!" He snorted in his beard. "*Civilians!*" There was infinite contempt in the way he spat out the word. Pedro, who until a week ago had been a civilian himself, felt abashed.

Twice more enemy war parties appeared, but were put to flight before they could come within range. After that the contingent saw no more of them. But other contingents evidently did, for from time to time a burst of arquebus fire would resound among the hills. The shots sent echoes bounding from ridge to ridge in overlapping bursts of sound. To Pedro, who never before had heard gunfire, the effect was both fearsome and fascinating.

Marcos spoke thoughtfully. "Gunpowder is making war too murderous to be practical. My guess is that these modern weapons will soon put an end to all wars everywhere, once and for all." A worried expression crossed his face. After gunpowder had made wars a thing of the past, what would become of soldiers like himself?

The contingent pushed on, demolished more hamlets, destroyed more crops, seized some grain and provisions left behind in the hurry of flight. As dusk came on, some of the chill from the heights descended into the valleys, and the troops halted for the night in a deserted village. There was no lingering around the supper fires. As soon as the meal was over and sentries posted, the tired men took shelter. Pedro spoke sleepily to Chico as they stretched out on the floor in one of the houses.

"If there's an attack tonight, don't wake me—I'm much too tired to fight."

Luckily there was no attack, and Pedro's sleep was uninterrupted. But it was not undisturbed. All night long he dreamed. Sometimes he was chasing Moors. More often, they were chasing him.

The troops were up at the first hint of dawn. Before moving on, they paid for their night's lodging by devastating the terraced fields outside the village. The sun was beginning to climb when they resumed their march. It hadn't climbed far before a high slope rose in their path, blocking any view of what might lie beyond. A guide, riding ahead to scout the vicinity, stood in his stirrups and peered warily over the summit of the rise. Suddenly he shouted, and beckoned eagerly.

"*Muchachos!* Meat on the hoof!"

The troops swarmed up the slope, looked where the guide was pointing, and saw a large herd of cattle not far away, driven by a handful of Moorish peasants. Soldiers and drovers sighted one another almost simultaneously. The soldiers let out an exultant yell. The drovers stared for a panic-stricken instant, then began running frantically back and forth, waving their arms and prodding with their long sticks, trying to hurry the slow-moving animals.

The soldiers rushed down on the herd like swooping hawks. The herdsmen took to their heels, their skimpy rags flapping as they scrambled to find hiding places among the tumbled rocks. They were out of sight before the Spaniards came up. A shouted order halted a few soldiers who started in search of them.

"Don't waste time looking for the wretches—it's the cattle we want."

The yelling and commotion had a predictable effect on the herd. Some of the frightened animals began to scatter, others milled about in an uneasy cluster. The troops circled around and gradually got the beasts under control, headed off in a new direction, bawling in protest.

The contingent leader managed to bawl even louder. "We'll rejoin the main force, men. They'll take over the cattle, and we can go ahead with our work."

By this time the order of march had been well shuffled, for troops can't maintain formation while rounding up cattle. Pedro blinked the sweat from his eyes and looked about in search of Chico. To his surprise, he found him in his customary place, right beside him, looking as unruffled as always. *Caray!* Pedro thought, the fellow isn't even breathing hard! Somewhere behind he could hear Marcos, his voice carrying like a trumpet blast through the din of the cattle.

Pedro had to regain some breath before he could speak. "I can think of pleasanter tasks than driving these bawling beasts. Let's hope the main force isn't far off."

Chico answered with characteristic unconcern. "It can't be far off, as a bird flies."

"I know. The trouble is, we're not birds."

As it happened, the main force was closer than Pedro had dared hope—only two hills and a hollow away. It had grown considerably, for other contingents had also rounded up droves of cattle and sheep, and seized stores of grain and other provisions. The captains were debating what to do about the accumulated plunder. There was too much to manage without slowing progress and hampering freedom of action. Even more important, the wounded men needed care, and in some cases the need was urgent. It was decided that a guard detachment should see the wounded and the plunder safely back to camp, while the bulk of the force continued the advance. As the force was being divided, a captain had an afterthought.

"Pick out some raw recruits to drive the cattle—they're little use as soldiers."

So it was that Pedro, as raw a recruit as any in the army, found himself heading back toward the camp, urging along a horde of bawling and bleating livestock. The same lowly task fell to Chico. The older men and experienced soldiers stayed with the main force, to carry out further forays. Marcos threw the two youths a friendly taunt as they moved off.

"See that you herdsboys get the cows home before dark."

Pedro grinned in response. He liked the big, genial soldier with that booming voice and deceptively fierce face.

Once they were on their way, Pedro caught only occasional glimpses of Chico, who was stationed well ahead of him. Anyone as short as Chico was easy to lose sight of. Pedro was none too happy about his new assignment. Herding cattle wasn't his idea of a proper job for a soldier. Even so, he decided, it was better than ravaging farms.

The procession wound among the hills. A guard division marched in advance and another brought up the rear. Between them were the wounded, the pack animals laden with captured stores, and the sheep and cattle. The wounded who were unable either to walk or to stay in a saddle were carried on makeshift stretchers.

An hour or so passed with no sign of the enemy. Then a body of horsemen appeared over a distant ridge, but the formidable size of the guard evidently gave them pause, and they lingered but briefly before dropping back out of sight. Later, bursts of gunfire sounded from distant points, indicating that yesterday's attacks were being renewed. Pedro heard them with a curious lack of concern; already he was becoming inured to a danger which was constantly present.

His mind was mainly occupied with his task. He ranged back and forth along the flank of the herd, occasionally urging a reluctant beast with the butt of his pike, now converted into a prod stick. It was a question which made more noise, the drovers or the herd. Pedro added his own strong voice to the din.

The herders were strung out at fairly close intervals, but there wasn't much friendly conversation—most of their remarks were addressed to the cattle, and weren't at all friendly. But Pedro struck up an acquaintance with the youth just ahead, who fell back from time to time long enough to exchange a few words. He was a slim, loose-jointed fellow, not much older than Pedro but a full head taller. Wrinkled hose encased his lanky legs, a sleeveless, open-fronted jerkin flapped over his shirt, and a bright-colored kerchief—customary headgear in southern Spain—was wound about his head.

"Francisco Torres," he said, introducing himself. "Paco, to my friends. My enemies too, for that matter. I'm new to the army. You too, I suppose?"

"I was new a week ago. Not any more." Pedro grinned.

"Um, you're right—we're not so new at that. After all, we've been under fire." Paco thoughtfully scratched his head through his kerchief. "And to think that just two weeks ago I was trying to get permission to enlist."

"I suppose you got it?"

"No. As a matter of fact, I didn't. My father wouldn't hear of it—said I'm too young to be a soldier. Too young! And here I am seventeen!"

"What did you do—run away?"

"Oh, no. I wouldn't defy my father like that. I just told him I was going—and I went."

While Pedro was turning this over in his mind, Paco shouted suddenly and bounded forward to poke a lagging animal. Pedro was having trouble with his charges too. A venturesome heifer kept straying from the herd, seemingly convinced that the more distant herbage was tastier than that along the line of march. No sooner would Pedro get it back into the fold than it was off again in search of greener pastures.

Presently Paco fell back into step with him and resumed their interrupted talk. "Contrary beasts, aren't they? Noisy, too. Oh, by the way, what did you say your name is?"

Pedro didn't recall mentioning his name, but he supplied the information and added a few details about his background. Paco seemed fascinated.

"A monastery! Imagine that! And now you're a soldier. Sorry you made the change?"

"Of course not. I love La Rábida, but I wouldn't want to stay there all my life."

"I know what you mean. That's just the way I felt about *my* home. And besides, I hated the work I was doing. It was so dull, so boring."

"What kind of work were you doing?" Pedro asked.

"I helped my father. He worked for a cattle-raiser. That's why I joined the army—to get away from herding cattle." And Paco threw back a rueful grin as he bounded forward to cope with another recalcitrant charge.

The cavalcade moved along, hoofbeats and footfalls raising swirls of dust that shimmered in the air like thin gauze, and stuck in the throat like thick wool. It was midafternoon now, and the heat of the sun was making itself noticed. Pedro slid his tunic off his shoulders and let it hang from his belt so he could feel a breeze through his shirt. There being no breeze, it didn't help much.

He was still having trouble with the self-willed heifer, whose soul seemed charged with wanderlust. Pedro looked up from a moment's inattention to see it some distance away, sampling the tufts of grass that edged a high rocky outcrop. In that moment he understood why Satan's imps were always pictured with horns, tails, and cloven hoofs.

"Why, you stupid, contrary. . . ." Pedro searched his vocabulary for a suitably expressive word. Having been reared in a monastery he found none. He started toward the animal, then, realizing that a direct approach would only drive it farther astray, circled on a wide detour in order to close in from behind.

The heifer stopped cropping grass and eyed Pedro warily. Pedro, eying the heifer just as warily, continued his circuit. The heifer, seeing his intention, promptly moved around the shoulder of rock and down the slope which dropped off beyond. Pedro, determined not to be out-maneuvered, also moved down the slope and began to close in. He had taken just a few steps when a shadow of movement drew his eyes back to the jutting rock. Suddenly he forgot all about the heifer. His heart leaped into his throat.

Scarcely a dozen paces away, pressed close against the projection of rock, was a robed and turbaned Moor!

Pedro's throat worked as he tried to summon his voice. After a moment he managed to call out, but amid the noise of the herd his shout was lost like a whisper in a storm. He waved his hand wildly to attract his companions' attention, and realized with dismay that both he and the Moor were hidden by the outcropping of rock. He gulped. Then he gripped his pike more firmly and leveled it menacingly toward the Moor. It would have looked even more menacing had he leveled it point-forward. Having used it to prod cattle, Pedro had the business end behind him.

"Make one move and it'll be your last." The fierce threat lost much of its effect because his voice *would* quaver. He hoped his attitude conveyed his meaning, even though the Moor probably didn't understand a word of Spanish.

And then Pedro's wits, scattered by surprise, began to reassemble. The Moor was making no hostile move. Indeed, he could scarcely hold himself upright, and was using the rock as a support. There was a great red stain on the shoulder and sleeve of his robe. And his clothing was in shreds, covered with dirt.

Pedro felt a surge of pity and lowered his pike. Enemy or not, this man needed help. He started forward, then hesitated as he came nearly in reach of the Moor. The man was watching him, pain and exhaustion plain in his face. Now he spoke, his voice weak and gasping.

"*Compañero!* Comrade! Help . . . me."

Pedro's mouth fell open. "You speak Spanish!"

The other drew a long breath, and his voice gained momentary strength. "I . . . I *am* Spanish. Help me, lad. I'm. . . ."

The man staggered suddenly, clutched desperately at his rocky support, then slid to the earth.

The Queen's Hospital

Pedro sprang forward to help the stranger, who was clawing at the rock in an effort to pull himself upright. As gently as he could, Pedro got him on his feet and, staggering under his weight, moved back up the slope toward the cavalcade. One of the drovers saw them coming and pointed excitedly.

"Look—a Moor! The lad's captured a Moor!"

Several men came running to help Pedro with his burden. A captain up forward looked around, stared briefly, then spurred his mount to the spot.

"What's this, lad? You've taken a Moor?"

"Not a Moor, sir," Pedro panted. "He's a Spaniard."

"A Spaniard? In those clothes? How do you know?"

"Why. . . ." Pedro suddenly realized that he *didn't* know. It hadn't occurred to him to doubt the stranger's statement. The wounded man looked up at the captain.

"I . . . am Spanish." The words came faintly between gasps for breath. "Held captive in Granada. . . . Escaped yesterday. . . ." His voice trailed off and he clutched at his blood-stained shoulder, his face twisting in pain.

"Don't try to talk now, *amigo*," someone advised him. "You can explain after—Ay! The poor devil's fainted." The wounded man had sagged forward, his head lolling on his chest.

They eased him to the ground and peeled down the bloodied robe, exposing an ugly wound where an arquebus ball had plowed through his upper arm, just by the shoulder joint. It had bled profusely, and partially dried blood smeared his arm and chest. A soldier ran to one of the pack animals and hurried back with a wineskin and a packet of bandages. He proceeded to wash the wound in the strong spirits, then bandaged it crudely. Pedro, meanwhile, was giving the captain the details of what had happened.

The officer studied the wounded man. "He's probably telling the truth, but we can't learn anything further now. His story can be checked at camp, when he's able to talk."

The soldier who was bandaging the wound straightened. "That's all that can be done now. We'll have to make another stretcher." He turned to Pedro, who was nearest. "Here lad, let's have that pike."

Pedro handed it over, wondering vaguely how he'd ever managed to hold on to it while supporting the wounded man. Another man also surrendered his weapon, and the stranger's robe was stretched between the two shafts to fashion a makeshift stretcher. The wounded man moaned as he was placed upon it, then lay still, eyes closed and breath coming in hoarse gasps.

Pedro, feeling responsible both for his pike and for the stranger, became one of the stretcher-bearers. He still wasn't sure whether he had rescued a friend or captured an enemy. In either case it was something of an exploit, and questions pelted him from all sides as the cavalcade got under way again. Pedro made the most of his sudden importance and recounted the adventure in full detail.

His nerves were still pleasantly aquiver from the experience. It struck him that it wouldn't have happened at all, but
for a wayward heifer. That perverse beast, seeing that its
rambling was drawing no more attention, had rejoined the
herd of its own accord and was plodding docilely along with
the rest of the cattle.

One of the forward stretcher-bearers glanced around at his
inert burden with suspicion in his face. "If he was running
away from Granada, how did he get wounded? My guess is
that he was with one of those Moslem war parties."

The bearer paired with Pedro shook his head. "He's not a
soldier—at least he isn't in military dress."

"*Hombre!* Neither am I, but I'm a soldier, nonetheless.
Anyway, his boots have a military look. Boots, mind you!
Captives don't wear boots—they're lucky if they're given a
pair of worn-out sandals." The suspicious one threw another
glance at the wounded man. "I say he's no Spaniard. But I
hope I'm wrong—I'd hate to think I'm straining my back
lugging a heathen Moslem."

Pedro, carrying the rearward end of the shaft, looked down
at the man on the stretcher. "Heathen Moslem" seemed an
accurate description. The man's turban framed a lean face,
smooth-shaven except for a thin mustache curving around
the lips and a small tuft of beard in the center of the chin.
The nose was slightly aquiline, the cheekbones prominent
but finely modeled. His skin was a dark olive, almost
swarthy, but pallor showed underneath—plainly he had lost a
great deal of blood. He looked to be in his early twenties.

Pedro's eyes moved on down the supine form. The man's
torso was slim, well-knit but not muscular. The loose-fitting

trousers were torn and dirt-stained, as if he had dragged himself through rock and brush for a long distance; the boots, calf-length and curve-toed in the Moorish fashion, were scuffed and dusty. But the trousers and boots looked to be of good quality, and Pedro began to share something of the forward-bearer's suspicion.

"He does look well-dressed for a captive," he observed dryly.

The bearer beside him responded. "Captives *are* well-dressed if they're lucky enough to be attached to a wealthy lord's household. That happens sometimes."

Yes, sometimes, Pedro thought. But not many captives were so fortunate—most were locked in dungeons for ransom, or sent to the mines, or chained to galley oars. He looked again at the stranger's face. It was expressionless, save when it twitched in pain as the stretcher lurched and jolted. The man's eyes were closed, but Pedro felt sure he wasn't unconscious, and might well be listening to the bearers' comments.

With no stops to ravage farms or fight Moors, progress was comparatively rapid on this return journey, and the sun had not set when they reached the outlying ridges of the mountain range. The camp and the city came into view. The sun's last rays lengthened the tents' pointed shadows into spear shapes, leveled menacingly toward Granada. A city of canvas menacing a city of stone!

He glanced down again at the stranger and saw that his eyes were open, darting back and forth between the city and the camp. Suddenly the man looked up and met Pedro's eyes. There was a flicker of recognition and the faintest hint of a smile, then his eyes closed again. But Pedro was certain now that the man knew what was going on. He wondered what thoughts were hidden behind those closed lids.

It was dark when the cavalcade reached the camp, and lanterns and torches had been lighted. Men came hurrying from all sides, eager to learn what had happened in the mountains. The man in Moorish dress aroused instant curiosity, and a crowd came along as he and the other wounded men were taken to the hospital compound. On the way, the returning troops traded experiences with those who had remained in camp. Out of the confused babble Pedro gathered that nothing interesting or exciting had happened here.

"The Moors haven't so much as showed a turban," announced the voice nearest him. "You fellows had all the excitement, out there in the mountains. Here in camp it was dull as dust. Oh, we saw action, all right—clearing away brush, unloading equipment, building corrals for livestock. Yes, indeed, plenty of action. Hah! There's the hospital compound, just ahead. We finished setting it up just before sundown. Barely in time, eh?"

Torches set on high poles revealed the six huge tents which comprised the hospital compound. Only one of the tents was lighted from inside, and scurrying shadows on the canvas walls told of activity within. The crowd fell back as the wounded men were taken to the illuminated tent. Pedro looked about with interest as he entered. He gathered a swift impression of half-unpacked boxes, a double row of cots and a number of bustling figures, then he and the other bearers moved on to the far end of the tent, where wooden slabs were hurriedly being placed across trestles to serve as surgical tables. As soon as a table was set up, a wounded man was placed upon it. A low moan broke from the stranger's lips as he was lifted to one of the tables.

The other bearers left without loitering, seemingly glad to be gone. Pedro realized that he should do likewise, for he'd be in the way here. But as he started to pick up his pike, an orderly touched his arm.

"Sit there and wait until we finish with the worst cases." He motioned to a bench where a handful of men were seated, waiting to have minor injuries looked after.

Pedro was surprised at the order, but glad to obey. Wearily he sank down on the bench, grateful for a chance to rest. The orderly's face was puzzled as he sponged off the dried blood around the stranger's wound. Pedro saw his puzzlement and managed a tired grin.

"Don't worry—he's a Spaniard. It's only his clothes that are Moorish. At least, that's what he told us." And he gave a quick account of what had happened.

A surgeon came up, followed by his young apprentice carrying a tray laden with drugs, ointments, and surgical instruments. Pedro eyed the implements with mingled interest and distaste. There were forceps and scalpels of various sizes, and of course scissors and razors. These last were the most frequently used, for nearly all surgeons of that day were barbers by trade. They dressed wounds, set fractured bones, and pulled teeth as a sideline to shaving and haircutting.

The surgeon had a brisk, competent air which suggested, rightly or wrongly, that he knew his business. Removing the bandage on the stranger's arm, he examined the injury. "Hmm-m-m. The ball went clean through. That's good—we won't have to probe." Then he shook his head grimly. "It's been left untended too long—much too long."

The stranger's face tautened in pain as the injury was cleaned and treated. He gave an agonized cry when the hot iron was applied to cauterize the wound, then he sank into a merciful unconsciousness. He was still in a comatose state when, the wound again bandaged in wine-soaked cloths, he was transferred to one of the cots.

The surgeon now gave his attention to the men less seriously hurt. When each had been treated, bandaged, and assigned to a cot, he turned with an air of impatience to Pedro, still seated on the bench.

"Well, lad, what are you waiting for? Get out of your shirt and let's have a look."

Pedro stared in astonishment, but he was soldier enough not to question an order. He started to take off his shirt, but paused abruptly as his eyes fell on the reddish-brown smear near the top of the sleeve, scarcely noticed until now. Suddenly he understood why the orderly had directed him to wait. He looked at the surgeon in confusion.

"I'm not wounded, sir—that's *his* blood on my shirt." He gestured toward the stranger. "You see, I helped him get up on his feet, and he was bleeding so, and. . . ." His embarrassed shrug completed the explanation.

The surgeon seemed undecided whether to look sheepish, irritated, or amused. He made a sound in his throat which might have been a chuckle. "Well, now that you're here, you can lend a hand cleaning up this mess. *Madre mia!* Wounded to look after before we're half organized!" He shook his head testily and turned away.

Pedro groaned inwardly. He was tired to his very bones, but an order is an order, so he stumbled forward to help the men who were clearing away the unsightly litter where the wounded had been treated. Just then another surgeon passed, wiping red-smeared hands on a red-smeared apron. He looked at Pedro keenly, then stopped him.

"Never mind the work, lad—it's near done now. You're near done too, from the look of you. Find yourself a place to sleep, and you can make yourself useful in the morning. We're going to need some extra help getting the place properly set up."

Pedro gave him a grateful smile, surprised to find that even a surgeon might have a kind heart. Pedro shared the attitude of his time toward surgeons. As a class they were looked upon as something necessary but not quite respectable. Physicians enjoyed a somewhat higher esteem.

Looking about for a sleeping place, he spied a canvas-covered stack of pallets, not yet unpacked. Pausing only long enough to kick off his shoes, he fell upon the stack in a limp sprawl. He drew a long, tired sigh. The two days just past had been eventful enough to satisfy all thirst for excitement for some time to come. His eyes were heavy, but he kept them open long enough for a final look around the tent.

Pedro had heard of this hospital often. The "Queen's Hospital," it was called, for the Queen had conceived the idea and provided funds to keep it going. Military hospitals were not unknown, but a mobile medical unit which could accompany an army into the field was something new. The Queen's Hospital was staffed with experienced surgeons and apothecaries, and equipped not only with medical and surgical aids, but with comforts seldom enjoyed by soldiers, such as cots and sheets.

He was lucky, Pedro told himself, to be living in this advanced age—this Year of Our Lord 1491—rather than in some benighted era of the past.

Despite his weariness, or perhaps because of it, sleep was elusive. Even after the activity subsided he remained vaguely aware of quiet movements, of the heavy breathing, and occasional moans of wounded men. It must have been past midnight when sounds from one of the cots brought him fully awake. Someone was stirring restlessly and muttering, apparently with fever. At first the incoherent phrases made little impression on Pedro, then something unfamiliar in their sound caught his attention. The words weren't Spanish, but Arabic. He didn't understand that language, but he'd heard it often enough to recognize it—with Spanish and Moorish territories adjoining, there had been considerable intermingling of blood and language.

Pedro raised himself on an elbow and looked about. The lanterns had been dimmed to mere flickers, but he could see the outlines of the cots and their occupants. It was the stranger who was muttering, his voice thick with delirium. Pedro settled back and lay listening, fresh suspicion stirring in his mind. Presently the feverish murmur subsided, but Pedro was still vaguely wondering as he again drifted toward sleep.

Now at last he slept soundly, and when he woke again it was morning and the tent was stirring into life. As soon as he opened his eyes he looked toward the stranger's cot. The man appeared to be sleeping, the fever evidently gone with the night. Pedro studied him at length. Without the turban he looked less like a Moor—probably, Pedro thought, he was just what he claimed to be, an escaped Spanish captive. Still, it would seem that a delirious man would speak in his native tongue.

Oh, well, it wasn't *his* concern. The authorities would doubtless settle the question one way or the other.

He got up. For a moment he stood undecided, wondering where he should report for duty, since his unit was still absent in the mountains. A hospital orderly made the decision for him. "Here's a broom," he said pleasantly but pointedly. "I'm sure you want to pay for your night's lodging."

Pedro plied the broom with enough diligence to pay for the night's lodging and for the morning's breakfast as well. The hospital was well supplied with basins and hot water, so he borrowed time from the work to wash off the dust and sweat he'd brought back from the mountains, and while he was about it, scrubbed the bloodstain from his shirt. Then he went to the adjoining tent to help set up cots, and after that lent a hand to unpacking supplies. His fellow workers were soldiers like himself, detailed to get the six hospital tents ready for use.

Pedro welcomed the work. It brought him into contact with an unfamiliar and interesting part of the army, and besides, he hoped to learn something about the stranger while he was here. An avid curiosity had taken hold of him. Be the man Moor or Spaniard, he must have an exciting story to tell, and Pedro was itching to hear it.

When the work took him back into the main tent, an orderly thrust a bundle of torn and blood-stiffened clothes at him. "Take these out and burn them. They're good for nothing else—not even mop-up rags."

Pedro recognized the stranger's clothing in the bundle. As he fed the garments one by one to the fire he examined them with interest. What a difference between Moorish and Spanish clothes, he thought. The long band which wound into a turban vaguely suggested an Andalusian headkerchief, but the baggy trousers were completely unlike the close-fitting, waist-high hose which encased Spaniards' legs. And the long Moorish outer robe resembled neither an up-to-date doublet nor an old-fashioned tunic. As he examined the robe, the man who was tending the fire noticed his interest.

"It's called a 'burnous,' " the man told him. "Quite serviceable it is—heavy enough to be warm but loose enough to be cool. And the hood can either be drawn over the head for shade, or you can let it hang as a carry-all for small articles."

Pedro laughed. "Clever, these Moors! Maybe we ought to borrow some of their ideas."

"We already have—plenty of them," the other said. And he threw more wood on the fire, for it had to be kept at a high blaze to insure the hospital of a constant supply of hot water.

When Pedro went back into the tent he saw that the stranger was awake, looking rested and more alert. Pedro approached the cot, hoping the man was able to talk now. When the stranger saw him, a gleam of recognition lighted his eyes.

"You're the lad who rescued me, aren't you?" His voice was weak, but warm and friendly. "I owe you my deepest gratitude."

"You owe me nothing," Pedro said, eagerly coming up close. "I'm more than glad I happened to see you. But even if I hadn't, the troops would have rescued you."

The man shook his head. "No, they'd have passed by without even knowing I was there. I couldn't have dragged myself past that rock. I kept calling out, but I couldn't make myself heard."

"No wonder. That bleating and bellowing would have drowned out the noise of a battle." Pedro paused and cast about for something to say. He was bursting with curiosity, but he could hardly start plying the man with questions the moment the conversation opened. Then he remembered that he hadn't introduced himself. "By the way, my name is Pedro Tegero," he volunteered.

He waited expectantly, but the other didn't respond at once. He lay silent so long that Pedro wondered whimsically if he was trying to remember his name. At last he said slowly, "My name is Felipe." There was another long pause; then he added, "Felipe Luza."

He seemed suddenly to find it difficult to talk, or perhaps was unwilling to. Pedro made a hopeful attempt to keep the conversation going, but the man's tired manner wasn't encouraging, so he desisted.

"Perhaps you'd better rest now, Felipe," he said. "I hope I haven't tired you."

"Not at all, Pedro," the other said, but his appearance belied the words.

Pedro made a parting remark and turned away. When he glanced back, Felipe's eyes were closed again.

Having learned nothing about the man except his name,

Pedro was still keenly curious. Their brief talk had given him
a favorable impression of his new acquaintance. Felipe was
no Moor, Pedro assured himself. A Moor, even a grateful
Moor, would surely show some sign of hostility. And his
speech wasn't accented. He was dark, true, but so were many
Spaniards. And yet, why that long pause before telling his
name? It was just the way a Moor might pause if he had to
assume a Spanish name on the spur of the moment. But
then, it was also the way a man will pause when he's sick and
in pain, and talking wearies him.

Pedro shook his head uncertainly. The signs seemed to
point both ways at once.

After the noonday meal he was again sent to another tent,
where he worked through the afternoon. By evening all six
tents had been stocked and furnished, and after supper the
work detail was dismissed. Before leaving, Pedro went back
to the main tent and got his pike, which he'd stowed in a
corner where it wouldn't get lost in the clutter. On his way
out he paused by Felipe's cot. Felipe's eyes were closed, but
Pedro felt sure he wasn't asleep. His face had an intent,
tight-set look, perhaps from physical pain. But to Pedro it
hinted equally at mental concentration, as if some deep problem absorbed his mind.

"Are you still here?" demanded a waspish voice at his elbow. Pedro turned to see the surgeon who had ordered him
to work the night before.

"I'm leaving right now." And Pedro did leave—hurriedly,
lest the order be repeated.

Outside, he slowed up a bit and went in search of Chico.
He must visit Felipe often, he resolved, reflecting piously on

what he'd learned in the monastery—that to visit the sick is a meritorious act of mercy. Then his honest nature asserted itself and he grinned inwardly. Why try to fool himself? It wasn't Christian charity that prompted the noble resolve—it was plain, snoopy curiosity.

A Dream Is Born

Pedro's day-long stay in the hospital had in a sense been un-authorized, and he expected to have some explaining to do. But with his unit officers away in the mountains, there was no one to explain to. The camp was still only half organized. Irregularity was the rule. Oh, the nobles' regiments fell out on parade as was proper, all spit and polish. But the common soldiers had work to do, and it didn't seem to matter who was working where, as long as everybody was working.

And everybody was working. The men who had brought the cattle back from the mountains were now wielding picks and shovels, barricading the camp with trenches and earth-works. They didn't question Pedro about his absence. They hadn't even missed him. It made him feel very insignificant as he set to work with them the next morning. Chico was be-side him as usual, and as they dropped down into a half-finished trench, shovels in hand, a lanky figure stepped down at his other side. It was Paco. With no preliminary, he re-sumed the conversation they had begun on the way back from the mountains.

"*Madre mia!* I joined the army to get away from herding cattle. And look at me now—a ditchdigger." Paco swung his pick and bit a chunk of earth from the bank of the trench.

Then he straightened and fetched a lugubrious groan. "Yes, that's why I left home. I hated the sight of cattle. *Ay!* When I get back I'm going to give every cow in the pasture a great big kiss."

Pedro grinned. "Those cows will have to wait for their kisses. We're digging in for a long stay here."

"Don't remind me. I'm trying to be brave." And Paco fetched another groan. Pedro wasn't sure whether he was joking or not. Probably Paco wasn't sure either.

The morning passed quickly. The work was hard, but there was plenty of company to make it seem easier. A constant babble of voices mingled with the thud and scrape of picks and shovels. The men's earlier tension was gone now, but they still looked often toward Granada, a questioning wariness in their eyes. An armed and armored unit was always on duty, alert for any sign of enemy activity. No movement could be detected in the city. It remained silent, tomblike, its massive gates closed.

Midday brought a pause in the work for a rest and a light meal. Pedro turned yet again toward Granada, looking past the encircling walls to the hill rising above them in the heart of the city. Groves and gardens laid a green carpet on the slopes, and on the summit, crowning the height like a huge stone diadem, stood an imposing mass of red-toned walls and towers. The Alhambra! Palace and fortress, where a long line of proud monarchs had ruled a vast kingdom. Now the towers looked down on the last pitiful remnant of that kingdom, bounded by the city's walls.

"They say there's no more beautiful palace in the world than the Alhambra," Pedro remarked. "All we can see from here is a shell. Inside it's magnificent, they say. Courts and fountains and gardens, and hundreds of rooms." He shook his head wonderingly. "Imagine living in a place like that!"

"It wouldn't be cramped, that's sure," Paco said lightly. Then his manner sobered. "Yes, Boabdil lives in luxury, but I don't envy him. Not at a time like this."

"Maybe he's looking down at the camp right now," Pedro said. "I wonder what he's thinking, what plans he's making."

"Who knows?"

Both looked long and thoughtfully at the Alhambra's red towers. Chico's eyes followed theirs. For a brief moment he looked at the imposing pile with no visible interest. Then, without a change of expression, he turned his attention back to his bread and cheese.

The next afternoon the expedition came back from the mountains. The laborers paused in their work to watch its arrival. Apparently there had been few casualties. A handful of men wore red-stained bandages, but none needed a stretcher. There was plunder aplenty. The pack animals were all but hidden under loads of grain and provisions, and a multitude of cattle and sheep raised an incessant uproar. Pedro's eyes went wide when he saw two captive Moors behind the herd, choking in its dust. Their hands were bound, their clothes bedraggled, but their bearded faces glared defiance. Catching sight of Marcos in the procession —that giant frame would be hard to miss—Pedro snatched off his stocking-cap and waved. The response was a genial bellow that carried above even the noise of the herd.

Pedro hurried off in search of information as soon as work

halted. He saw Marcos in a group by one of the roasting pits. Pedro hesitated at the edge of the group, for a fledgling soldier doesn't burst uninvited into a gathering of veterans. But when Marcos saw him and boomed a greeting he moved up close and let fly with eager questions.

Nothing had happened worth the telling, Marcos assured him. A few light skirmishes, that was all. Those captured Moors? Oh, they were just careless—Moorish cavalrymen should know better than to let their horses get shot from under them. However, they had been persuaded—none too gently, Pedro gathered—to confide something of the situation in Granada.

Marcos shrugged. "They told us nothing that we couldn't have guessed. What it amounted to was just that Boabdil isn't going to surrender in a hurry, whatever the odds."

"What does he intend to do?" Pedro asked.

"What *can* he do? He's too proud to surrender, and too outnumbered to fight. Which means that we're in for a long, monotonous seige, just as I've said all along."

Pedro made a wry face. "*Ay!* I'd rather take my chances in battle than die of boredom. You think we'll see no action at all?"

Marcos was a long time answering. He glanced toward the city, his flint-hard face unreadable. At last he said slowly, "Don't be too eager, Pedro. We may see more action than we've stomach for before this thing is settled."

The next day, another detachment set out to make further forays in the mountains. Pedro felt no envy as he watched the columns move off. He'd had enough of ravaging farms, he told himself. He'd had enough of digging trenches too, he

added, flexing his tired muscles. He hadn't anticipated either
task when he volunteered for army service. He had pictured
himself constantly battling with Moors and performing
heroic deeds and having glorious adventures. It hadn't occurred to him that there would be much more sweat and toil
than thrill and glory.

But army life had its pleasant aspects too. There were new
friends, and laughter and banter around the supper fires, and
the older soldiers' yarns to listen to. These older soldiers
weren't grizzled ancients, by any means—men barely turned
twenty often had years of battle experience behind them.
Pedro was fascinated by their tales of earlier battles and
sieges. Almería. Ronda. Moclín. Málaga. Baza. These had
been only names to Pedro—familiar names, associated with
stirring events, but still only names. To these men they recalled vivid personal experiences in camps and on battle-
grounds.

"*Caramba!* I could listen all night to those fellows," Pedro
exclaimed, as he and Chico settled themselves for sleep after
one of the nightly rounds of reminiscences. They were still
sleeping in the open—the tents were for the nobles and their
regiments, and the common soldiers had no shelters as yet.
"Those stories make me feel as if I were actually there—I
can almost see those battles being fought."

Chico yawned. "I can't."

The indifferent response failed to dampen Pedro's enthusiasm. "You know, we may have some stories to tell too, by
the time the war's over. Just think, Chico! We're watching
the last days of the last city of the Moorish kingdom. That's
something we can brag about to our grandchildren."

"We haven't got any grandchildren."

Pedro let that statement pass unchallenged. "I wonder what the Moors will do after we take Granada. Maybe they'll go back where they came from—some of them, anyway."

"Where they came from? But they've always been here."

"Oh, no. Not always. They came from North Africa—or rather, their ancestors did. Over seven centuries ago." It occurred to Pedro that his friend, not having the advantages of a monastery upbringing, knew nothing of their country's tumultuous history. Perhaps he should remedy that lack. "You see, Chico, the Moors invaded Spain way back in— oh, I forget what year it was, but it was a long, long time ago. They overran the whole country at first. Then we started pushing them back, little by little, until at last the only territory they still held was here in the south. Of course, it wasn't all continuous war—sometimes things would quiet down and both sides would live in peace for a while. But it was always a sort of shaky peace."

Pedro paused and waited for a comment, but there was none. He went on. "That's how things stood when you and I were born. And then about ten years ago the war broke out again and— But you know about that. We've been biting off Moorish territory a piece at a time—and now there's only Granada left."

Again Pedro paused and waited for a response. One came —a soft and peaceful snore. Pedro grinned in the darkness. It seemed that his history lesson had been wasted.

The more urgent work was finally finished. The encampment was securely entrenched. Powder and ammunition were stored in underground arsenals. Supplies and equipment were under canvas. The nobles and their regiments were comfortably settled in their colorful tents. Now at last the troops had time to think about shelters for themselves.

No tents were provided for the rank and file, of course. Tents for common soldiers? Not in that day! But the rank and file had learned to be resourceful. They built rude brush-thatched barracks, walled on three sides with branches and brushwood, the fourth side open. Building material came from the banks of the river that skirted the camp, and the demolished orchards in the vicinity. The shelters were quite small, the largest housing a dozen or so men, others only half that number.

Pedro broke into a chuckle as he eyed the unfinished structures, with their twiggy branches bristling every which way. "*Caray!*" he exclaimed. "They look like oversized bird's nests."

"Here's one bird who's ready for a nest right now." Paco let fall the tree limb he'd just dragged from the riverside and expelled his breath in a relieved whoof.

Chico came up with a huge armload of branches that almost hid his diminutive form. He dropped his burden and brushed some clinging twigs from his clothes. "Nearly finished," he observed, glancing at the shelters.

Paco nodded. "Yes. We'll be moving in by nightfall." He wiped his sweating face with the loose corner of the kerchief bound around his head. "Why don't we three try to get quarters together?"

"Why not?" Pedro said. Then he added a suggestion of his own. "Maybe we can get places with Marcos. He's sure to be one of the barrack-masters." An experienced soldier was assigned to each shelter as barrack-master, responsible for maintaining order.

The three borrowed time from their work to investigate, and found that Marcos did indeed have charge of a shelter. He boomed his willingness, and as soon as the walls were up the trio moved in. Two other soldiers, Andrés Camacho and Rodrigo Vargas, made an even half-dozen occupants, which was all the little structure had room for.

Andrés was a sad-eyed, glum-faced man, like Marcos a seasoned soldier, but with none of Marcos's vitality and friendliness. "Sour as a green apple," Paco observed to Pedro the next day. "He acts as if he's always thinking about a funeral —probably his own." Pedro had to agree. He was sure he could never learn to like the man. He was equally sure he'd have to learn to live with him.

Rodrigo was easy to like, a man in his mid-twenties who didn't speak much but had a quick and ready smile. His blue eyes and blond hair hinted that his ancestors had come from the northern province of Galicia, for dark coloring was the rule in sunny Andalusia. He had had a little army experience, having served in last year's campaign, but he was not a seasoned soldier.

It didn't take long for the six to get settled. Then a discussion arose as to what they should name their shelter, for all the barracks were being given names, prominently displayed for everybody to read. Not many of the men *could* read, but at least each knew what the letters on his particular shelter meant. There were descriptive names such as *La Caverna*— The Cave, or *La Caja*—The Box. And there were nonsensical names like *El Mirlo Blanco*—The White Blackbird, or *El*

Burro Borracho—The Drunken Donkey. Sometimes lots were drawn for the privilege of bestowing a sweetheart's name on a shelter, so there were quite a number of *Carmen*'s and *María*'s and *Alicia*'s. Some of the names had no meaning whatever, except possibly to the men who invented them.

The group considered and discarded several suggestions. Then Paco remembered Pedro's remark that the brushwood barracks looked like a bird's nest. He proposed that the shelter be named for what it resembled, and the others agreed. Since it was Pedro's remark which had inspired the name, it seemed fitting that he be allowed to prepare the label— "especially," Marcos pointed out, "since none of the rest of us can write." So a slab of wood, a brush, and a pot of paint were secured from the supply tent, and Pedro formed each letter with painstaking care, and the little structure proudly flaunted its new name—*El Nido*, The Nest.

Marcos made it clear right at the start that The Nest must be kept neat and clean, with each man's gear in each man's allotted space. "It may look like a bird's nest, but there'll be no loose feathers floating around," he declared, and though a grin was lurking behind his beard it was plain that he meant what he said.

When all the shelters were finished and christened and the litter of construction had been cleared away, the builders straightened aching backs, wiped sweaty faces, and surveyed the result. It was a city of brushwood, the shelters ranged in rows with military precision and sprucely-swept streets running between.

"Nothing fancy, but it'll do," Marcos boomed. "All it lacks is a few taverns."

The men sat late around the supper fires that night. There was more joking than grousing, and much swapping of yarns, and even a song or two. And then their mood grew mellow, and they spoke of their homes and their hopes, and there was scarcely a word about battles and sieges, and Pedro almost forgot that a hostile city was looming just a few miles away. The men were quieter than usual when at last they began dispersing to their various shelters.

Pedro and his barrackmates talked briefly as they waited for sleep, but their voices soon drowsed into silence. Pedro usually fell asleep quickly, but now he lay awake, wistful and pensive. The talk around the supper fires had taken an unaccustomed turn tonight; he had caught glimpses of hopes and plans which the men usually kept to themselves. Pedro had spoken little. He too had hopes and plans, but they were too close to his heart to be revealed to others. His dream was a private dream, never shared with anyone.

He lay wide-eyed, looking out through the unwalled front of a shelter, random thoughts drifting in and out of his mind. The thoughts merged into memories, turning back to a day six years before, when his dream had first begun to take shape. The muffled sounds from outside reached his ears unheard, the moonlit encampment was unseen. His memory wandered to other sounds, other scenes. . . .

It had started on a day when a tall stranger, leading a small boy by the hand, rang the bell at the monastery gate.

Pedro, at his lessons with the other students, had seen the
two through the window and watched them with interest
—at nine, Pedro had found interest even in such a common-
place occurrence. The friar who answered the bell led the
man and the child across the courtyard, and as they came
near, Pedro could examine them more closely. The man's
face was strongly modeled and inclined to ruddiness, his hair
was grizzled but showed traces of rust-red. The boy was obviously his son. The resemblance was strong—the same ruddy,
freckled face and a mop of hair as red as his father's had
doubtless once been. As they passed the open window Pedro
caught a fragment of the monk's words.

". . . a cold drink will refresh you both. And the little one
must be hungry—I'll get him something to eat. You must
both rest after that long journey. You're welcome to. . . ."

Just a passing traveler, Pedro thought, and turned back to
his lessons. He had forgotten the incident that evening when
he started making the rounds with a taper, for it was his turn
that week to see that the lamps were lighted. He almost
passed by the room which served as study and library, assum-
ing it to be unoccupied at that hour, but as he moved past
the open door he heard the familiar voice of Fray Juan Pérez,
the prior of the monastery. Looking in, he saw three men at
the table in the center of the room. Beside Fray Juan was another friar, Fray Antonio Marchena, whom Pedro knew only
by sight, as he was from another Franciscan monastery, visiting La Rábida on some business concerning the Order. The
third man, Pedro noted with surprise, was the tall stranger
he'd seen that afternoon. The three were bent over a large
sheet of paper outspread upon the table.

Pedro gave a diffident knock, and Fray Juan looked up inquiringly.

"Shall I light the lamp, Fray Juan?"

"Ah, it *is* getting dark." The friar looked about with a faintly surprised air, then nodded. "By all means, Pedro. I hadn't noticed how late it's getting."

As Pedro held the taper to the lampwick he stole a glance at the paper on the table, and his eyes lighted with interest as he saw that it was a map. To Pedro, even at nine, maps spelled adventure and the lure of far lands. As he turned away he noticed that the child was in the room also, almost lost in the shadows as he sat on the bench in the corner, legs curled under him, plainly on the point of falling asleep.

Pedro looked questioningly at Fray Juan. The friar evidently sensed the glance, for he looked up and smiled slightly as he noticed the small boy. He touched the stranger's arm.

"The little one is tired. We've been so engrossed in our talk that we quite forgot him." He turned to Pedro. "Take the child to the dormitory, Pedro, and tuck him in for the night. He's completely worn out."

Pedro took the boy in tow. As he left the room, the friar spoke again. "When you've put the little fellow to bed, bring another lamp, Pedro. I have a feeling we're going to be up quite late." He flicked a smiling glance at his two companions. "We'll need all the light we can get on a subject like this."

As he led the child away Pedro tried to strike up a conversation, partly to put the boy at his ease, partly to satisfy his own curiosity. He was surprised to find that the child spoke very little Spanish. He was too sleepy to talk anyway, and all

Pedro could gather was that his name was Diego. The boy was asleep the moment he was in bed.

When Pedro returned to the study the three men were still huddled over the map, so absorbed they seemed scarcely to notice him as he placed the second lamp on the table. He caught the last of a remark from Fray Juan.

". . . a sound theory. To me it seems quite reasonable— and, I might add, intriguing. Don't you agree, Fray Antonio?"

"I do indeed," the other friar said. Then he added thoughtfully, "The venture will be costly, of course."

"I'm well aware of that." This was the tall stranger speaking, and Pedro noticed that his Spanish was halting and strongly accented. "That's the whole difficulty, and unfortunately I know no one in Spain who might finance the project."

"Perhaps I can help you there," Fray Antonio said. "There are some men of means among my acquaintances, some of them close to the court. I can arrange introductions for you."

"I would be forever grateful, Fray Antonio." The stranger shook his head wonderingly. "To think that I merely stopped here to arrange a temporary home for little Diego! I never dreamed that—"

"Providence brought you here, my friend. You must stay on, of course, long enough for us to make the necessary arrangements."

Pedro suddenly realized that he was standing there still unnoticed. He moved away. But at the door he stopped and looked back. There was a fascinating air of mystery and excitement in the way the three men huddled over that map. And something about the tall stranger—his manner, his voice, the eager way his fingers moved over the map—held Pedro like a magnet. The boy hesitated, then stepped out of the room and drew back into the shadows beyond the doorway.

He had no business lingering there and he was courting a reprimand, or worse. Heaven only knew how many verses of Scripture he'd have to memorize if one of the friars should come upon him. But nothing short of force could have dragged Pedro away before he heard more. Only a little more, he eased his protesting conscience, as he strained his ears to catch the fragments of talk that reached him.

". . . need only cross the Ocean Sea to . . . the island of Cipango lies close beyond . . . ruled by the Grand Khan . . . palaces in Cathay. . . ."

The magic phrases conjured up magic images. Pedro didn't hear all that was said, and he didn't understand all that he heard. But he heard and understood enough to set his blood surging with excitement and longing. This tall stranger had a dream—a wonderful, glorious dream—and some spark of its wonder and glory reached the heart of the nine-year-old boy listening at the doorway.

And as time passed, the spark had grown into an ardent flame, until now, six years later. . . .

Pedro stirred. The lamplit doorway dissolved and in its place was the moonlit opening of the shelter; the trio's talk became the voices of passing sentries, just coming off watch.

His mind slid back into the present, but it was still filled
with the dream, and the image of the tall man who had
awakened it.

Even on that first night Pedro had felt a yearning to share
in the great adventure. The feeling had matured, but it
hadn't lessened. Pedro still burned with that same desire,
still held fast to the dream born on that day six years before,
when a tall stranger appeared at the monastery gate—a tall
stranger named Christopher Columbus.

The Moors' Challenge

Pedro had thought often of Felipe Luza during the busy period just past. Now at last there was an occasional breathing space, and he took advantage of one of them to visit the hospital. Eager to become better acquainted with Felipe, and expecting to find him on the way to recovery, he was shocked to learn that the man was in no condition to have visitors.

"He took a turn for the worse a day or so after he was brought here," an orderly told him. "If that wound had got prompt attention he'd probably be on his feet by now. As it was, it brought on fever. He's been in a coma one day and delirious the next."

Pedro frowned in concern. "But—but is he going to . . . ?"

"God only knows. It could go either way."

Pedro was dismayed by the news. He didn't really know Felipe, but he felt a special interest in him and hoped desperately for his recovery. What an ironic tragedy it would be if, after long captivity and a near-miraculous rescue, Felipe should die before even tasting freedom.

He didn't dwell on the somber thought. There were many other things to occupy his mind—sentry duty, for instance, and clean-up detail. And, of course, drills.

Veteran campaigners conducted the drills, which were aimed at whipping the young fledglings into something resembling soldiers. Pedro congratulated himself when he was assigned to Marcos's squad, but soon started wondering if he'd been so lucky after all. Marcos the drillmaster was a far different person from Marcos the comrade-in-arms. His good-nature came off like a cloak; his bellowed sarcasm almost withered the awkward novices in their tracks.

"*Tontos!* You call yourselves soldiers? *Diablos!* If you ever charge the enemy you'll trip over your own weapons."

Few of the recruits were much older than Pedro, many even younger. They handled pikes and pole-axes like city boys handling hoes, and when they tried to execute maneuvers Pedro instinctively ducked, lest he get an ear lopped off. And—he realized it with chagrin—he himself was as clumsy as any bungler in the squad.

Once the drills were over, Marcos's smile would flash from behind his beard and he would be his usual amiable self. He and Andrés sought the companionship of the older men when their duties allowed. Pedro was with Chico and Paco much of the time, both on and off duty, and Rodrigo spent most of his free time with some friends from his own town who were quartered near The Nest. But each day's end brought the six together in their little shelter. Ill-assorted as the group was, a swift intimacy sprang up among them, in which even the dour Andrés shared.

They quickly came to know something of one another's personal history. Rodrigo, the others learned, had a wife and a small son waiting for his return. His voice would fill with longing whenever he spoke of them. Andrés too was married

—Pedro wondered how in the world so morose a man had ever managed to acquire a wife. Paco, it seemed, had left a dozen sweethearts languishing when he joined the army—or at least that was his story. Marcos was a bachelor and declared emphatically that he intended to remain one.

"Married life isn't for me," he boomed, his trumpet-voice battering the brushwood walls. "I'm a soldier."

"So am I, but I've got a wife and family," Andrés said. "Four boys, four girls—that's the count so far." He seemed to be speaking with pride, but that sad voice of his made one uncertain whether to offer congratulations or sympathy.

"What about you, Chico?" Marcos queried. "Is there a *muchacha* in your young life?"

"Of course," Chico said in his matter-of-fact way. "Her name is Lola. She's quite pretty. And she likes me a lot."

"So I assume you're going to marry her when you get a bit older?"

"I suppose so—if she wants me to," Chico said placidly.

As the days passed, the camp gradually settled into an uneventful routine. The Moors apparently planned no action. Granada stood silent. The smoke of hearth fires, drifting skyward, was the only evidence of the life that stirred beyond the walls. Then something occurred which showed that defiance smoldered in the beleaguered city.

The drills had just ended, and the soldiers were leaving the drillfield when sudden shouts and pointing fingers drew all eyes toward the city. A handful of horsemen had emerged from the gates and were galloping toward the camp. Bored sentries snapped alert at the sight; the duty squadrons sprang into formation, weapons readied, peering past the horsemen to see if a host of others would follow. But there were only six, though they rode with the assurance of an army, mailed tunics showing under their back-flung cloaks, their turbaned helmets gleaming in the sun.

The troops watched and waited in puzzled excitement. The horsemen were within shouting distance before they reined to an abrupt halt amid spurts of red dust. Then one of them spurred his mount a little forward. His shout carried clearly to the encampment.

"We challenge you, Christian dogs!" The Moor's Spanish held only a hint of accent. "You show much prudence but little valor, huddled there in your camp. But perhaps among so many there are a few with spirit enough to test our Moorish steel. We are six only. Are there six among you—only six—who are not cowards?"

The Moor moved back among his companions and waited. The Spanish soldiers pressed toward the edge of the encampment to see what might develop. Pedro's heart was thumping his ribs with excitement. For some time there was silence on both sides, then the Moor again spurred forward.

"Must we come into your camp and drag you out by the ears? Are there not even six among you who are men rather than worms?"

This time there was a response. "We are coming, Moor. Surely you don't begrudge us time enough to get into our armor!"

Excitement surged higher. Eagerly the soldiers fell back to make way for the six mounted knights who had appeared, fully armed and armored. Proudly the knights rode through the crowd, their faces confident under their crested morions.

But before they reached the camp's border, a shouted command halted them.

"Stay in the camp, *caballeros*. Don Ferdinand's orders."

The command came from a cavalier who had just ridden up from the interior of the camp. He raised his hand in an authoritative gesture. "His Highness forbids anyone to accept any such challenge as this—we are encamped here to lay siege, not to stage jousting exhibitions."

A murmur of disappointment rose among the troops. The six knights hesitated, exchanging resentful glances. Then without a word they swung their mounts and rode back toward their quarters. The cavalier who had halted them turned toward the Moorish horsemen and shouted something, and Pedro realized with surprise that he was speaking in Arabic. His tone was forceful but courteous, and after a moment the Moors' spokesman responded in the same manner. Then, with a defiant flourish of scimitars, the six Moors wheeled and thundered back toward the city in a flurry of dust.

Marcos nudged Pedro and jerked a thumb toward the cavalier. "That's don Gonzalo de Córdova. He speaks Arabic as well as any Moor in Granada. You've probably heard of him."

Pedro's eyes lighted. "Who hasn't heard of don Gonzalo!"

He studied the cavalier with interest, taking in the lean, straight figure and the strong, sensitive features. The man's appearance matched his reputation, Pedro thought—Gonzalo de Córdova was well known both as a warrior and as a courtier, respected by his peers and his subordinates alike. Pedro whistled in admiration as he looked at the superb horse don

Gonzalo rode, a milk-white Barbary steed. Marcos guessed the reason for the whistle.

"Beautiful animal, eh? Don Gonzalo got that horse as a present, Pedro. And who do you think gave it to him? Boabdil himself!"

"Boabdil?"

"None other. Don Gonzalo and Boabdil have been friends for years. I rather think they still are, unofficially."

Andrés puckered his lips in disapproval. "Don Gonzalo has many friends among the Moors—far too many, to my way of thinking. He has picked up a lot of their habits, too. I've heard he even follows their custom of daily bathing."

"Not only that," Marcos boomed. "He's said to be fond of that Moorish drink—what's it called? Oh, yes—coffee."

"I've heard of coffee," Pedro said. "I wonder what it tastes like."

"How should I know? I'd never try the heathen drink. They say it's the color of burned leather. Probably tastes like it, too." Marcos made a wry face. Lifting his small wineskin from his belt, he held it high and squirted a thin stream into his mouth. Expert from long practice, he didn't miss a drop of the fire-sharp, acid-strong liquid. He smacked his lips appreciatively as he watched the cavalier wheel his mount and ride away. "Whatever I may think of coffee and daily baths, I still admire don Gonzalo."

From then on such incidents occurred frequently. Granada wasn't strong enough for all-out battle, but that hadn't pared a chip from the belligerence of her fighting men. Parties of Moorish knights—sometimes only two or three, sometimes a score or more—would gallop to within shouting distance and challenge their Spanish counterparts to single combat or group skirmish. Many Spanish knights would readily have accepted, but for the King's order forbidding it. It was a sensible order, Pedro thought, but some of the older men seemed to have reservations.

"Times are changing," Marcos observed. "Not so long ago such an order would have been unheard of. Two enemy knights could carve each other up properly, with no interference. All according to the rules of chivalry, mind you. Both armies would look on without making a move." He gave a half-amused, half-regretful shake of his head. "Chivalry is going out of fashion now that gunpowder has come in. But some of those prancing knights would like to hang on to it."

It was true, Pedro knew, that many of the older knights resented the introduction of gunpowder. And why did they resent it? Simply because it killed a noble and a commoner without proper distinction. To their minds, it was honorable to get killed by a sword or a lance, facing a foeman who was suitably highborn. But being blown to bits by a distant blast, set off by a soldier without even a "don" prefixed to his name . . . ! *Por los santos*—that was downright ungentlemanly!

Pedro's thoughts still turned frequently to Felipe Luza. He made another inquiry at the hospital and learned that Felipe's condition showed a slight improvement. "He *may* pull through," the orderly said. "He's got a strong constitution." From this dubious statement Pedro took what encouragement he could.

To Pedro, camp life was still new enough to be exciting.

There was plenty of fun and horseplay to season the work, and as for the drills and discipline—why, they were part of the excitement. The only thing he really hated was sentry duty, with its pacing back and forth over the same monotonous stretch, walking for hours without getting anywhere. But sentry duty came only at intervals, thank the saints, and could be accepted as one of life's unavoidable nuisances, like gnats and dust and the morning trumpets that always sounded just when sleep was at its coziest.

There were periods of leisure tucked into the round of drills and duties. Pedro spent much of his free time exploring the camp with Chico and Paco. The trio made an amusing picture as they strolled along together, their varied heights ranged in three graduated steps—"like a staircase," Marcos chuckled. Pedro complained that his neck got sore from constantly looking up to the tall Paco and down to the diminutive Chico.

The vast expanse of tented canvas held a constant fascination. It was laid out in rectangular shape, with streets running its length and breadth from border to border, separating the camps of the various armies—for the host encamped in the vega was an aggregation of many distinct armies. There were the regiments maintained by the King and Queen. There were the private armies of various nobles, often larger and better-equipped than the Sovereigns' regiments. There were the squadrons of the Holy Brotherhood, an organization charged in peacetime with maintaining law and order in villages and countrysides, but called into the Sovereigns' service during this time of war. There were the partly religious, partly military Orders of Alcántara, Calatrava and Santiago

—each an army in itself—founded centuries before to defend Christendom against all enemies. Besides all these there were the various provincial levies such as Pedro's own unit.

The general effect was overwhelming. Endless varieties of liveries and uniforms, fluttering standards emblazoned with heraldic devices, multicolored tents, flashing accouterments —all combined into a bewildering scene of animated pageantry.

But the camp had its less glamorous side too. There were great pens for the cattle and sheep and poultry which supplied the army with meat, and massive bins of grain and flour, and supply tents where other provisions were stored in casks and bales and bulging sacks. Throughout the camp there was constant activity. Spits turned and caldrons simmered. Smiths and armorers sweated over glowing forges. Countless men performed countless tasks, and there were horses everywhere, tethered beside tents or enclosed in stockades or carrying riders about their business. Trains of laden pack animals plodded incessantly into the camp, while other trains, their burdens unloaded, moved in the opposite direction.

Pedro was amazed at the prodigious quantities of supplies. "Where on earth does it all come from?" he wondered.

"From all over Spain, I suppose," Paco ventured. "They say it's the Queen who sees to getting supplies and arranges for their transportation. It must be a tremendous task for a woman."

"It'd be a tremendous task for a man!" Pedro exclaimed.

Many besides Pedro had marveled at the responsibilities which the Queen had assumed. Not only must the main

army be provisioned, but also the garrisons in the scores of
Moorish towns already conquered. Nor was it only a question
of procuring supplies—there was also the problem of transportation. The country wasn't made for wagons—everything
had to be borne by beasts of burden, over rugged mountain
terrain. The Queen had hired fourteen thousand pack animals for this purpose, and even for these sure-footed beasts
roads sometimes had to be cut through formidable rocky
barriers.

Pedro whistled in wonder at the thought of such complex
problems.

"Compared to what the Queen is doing, the King has no
worries at all. *Quiá!* All *he* has to do is fight battles!"

Units from various provinces were quartered in separate
sections of the camp, and by roaming from one to another
the trio could mingle with men from all parts of Spain.
When they mentioned this to Marcos he wagged his beard in
mock disapproval.

"What's this country coming to? Andalusians hobnobbing
with—with *foreigners!*" He made a little barking sound, half
snort, half chuckle. "*Diablos!* I've seen the time when the
mere sight of a man from another province was enough to
start a fight."

The statement wasn't far from the truth. The Moors
might have been defeated long before if the Spaniards had
only stopped fighting among themselves. Their country, once
a patchwork of independent kingdoms, was gradually emerg-
ing as a united realm, but old feuds were slow in dissipating,
and each province still despised the others. But they all de-

spised the Moors, and there's nothing like a common enemy to reconcile quarreling neighbors.

No section of the camp was more interesting to the three friends than the artillery ground. They stopped there often, but when one afternoon Pedro suggested another visit, Chico and Paco agreed readily. When they reached the place they found the usual curious idlers, mostly younger soldiers like themselves, for whom the giant guns held a half-fearsome fascination.

Even the impassive Chico showed a stir of interest as the three moved along the rows of cannons, mounted on heavy wooden frames, with balls of stone or iron piled beside them. "They're big," he observed.

"Monsters," Pedro agreed.

Paco was looking ahead, staring in exaggerated surprise. "Do you see what I see? An artilleryman—fraternizing with the infantry!"

It *was* something to stare at. Artillerymen were an exclusive lot, taken as a whole. This one was perched on a cannon, as proudly as if he owned it, surrounded by a number of youths who listened with flattering attention as he talked.

Pedro started forward. "Let's join the party. Maybe we'll learn something."

The artilleryman, gratified at having such an interested audience, was addressing it with gusto, describing the part played by the big guns in former campaigns.

". . . smashed into gravel, those walls were, after a few blows from our cannonballs. Towers toppled like heaps of pebbles. Buildings flattened into paving stones. And noise!

—did you ever hear a hundred thunders crashing at once? That's the kind of noise these little pets make. Why, I remember how it was at Ronda, when. . . ."

Chico had wormed his way to the front of the audience. He had to, if he wanted to see anything. He indicated the big gun and made a respectful request. "Please, would you mind explaining how it works?"

The man complied with an air of patronizing indulgence. "Why, you see, the barrel is balanced on those trunnions, so it can be raised and lowered for aiming. The ball is loaded into that breechblock, and when the cannoneer puts his light to the touchhole—*Blam!*" His hands swept up and out in a gesture both expressive and explosive.

The ring of attentive faces looked properly impressed. "*Caramba!*" someone exclaimed in an awed voice. "And it can smash a stone wall with just one shot?"

"Well-l, not *every* shot," the man admitted. He hesitated, reluctant to spoil the effect he had created. But honesty compelled him to go on, for he was a truthful fellow, even if he was an artilleryman. "The trouble is, you don't often hit what you're aiming at. The ball usually overshoots the mark, or falls short, or else goes wide one way or the other. And sometimes the charge is too weak and doesn't go off. And then sometimes it's too strong and the whole cannon blows up—we've lost some good artillerymen that way." He paused and looked thoughtful for a moment. Then his face brightened and he beamed at his audience proudly. "But it's a terror of a weapon when it *does* work."

Anticipation

Another party was coming back from the mountains. Pedro watched the mounted column move across the vega, trailed by a haze of dust. He saw no livestock or provisions. There wasn't much left to forage for now—the region had already been pretty well scoured—but squadrons of cavalry still went out at intervals to patrol the area. They reported no more skirmishes—evidently Boabdil was keeping his army within the walls to guard the city.

Well, thought Pedro, the cavalry was welcome to the job. It was a relief to know that he wouldn't be called upon to despoil any more farms. To be sure, he'd seen some excitement out there in the mountains—more than he'd seen in the nearly a month that had passed since. For one thing, he'd taken part in battle action—well-l, skirmishes, anyway. And he'd distinguished himself by rescuing a captive.

That reminded him of Felipe. It lacked an hour or so until supper, and the time was his own. This would be a good chance to ask after Felipe again. Never one to waste opportunity, Pedro set out briskly for the hospital.

When he got there he heard good news. Felipe's condition showed marked improvement. "He's past the crisis now and on the road to recovery," an orderly told him.

"Thank the saints!" Pedro exclaimed, somewhat surprised at feeling such vast relief. After all, he hardly knew Felipe.

"Once he started, he improved fast," the orderly said. "Frankly, I didn't think he'd pull through at first. That was a bad wound, and it went untended for a full day. And just to think he got it from a Spanish arquebus! Devilish luck, getting shot by someone on your own side."

"He *is* Spanish, then?" Pedro asked eagerly.

"Of course. Don Gonzalo de Córdova questioned him and accepted his story—and he couldn't have deceived don Gonzalo. It seems he's been a captive for years. Then he finally managed to escape, only to get shot before he could reach our camp. Tck, tck—what a rotten twist of fortune!"

"May I see him now?"

"Not yet. Maybe in a week or so."

"But don Gonzalo—"

"I can't deny permission to don Gonzalo. To you I can." The orderly grinned and made a gesture of dismissal.

Pedro returned the grin and headed back toward The Nest. It was good to know that Felipe was recovering. And what a relief it was to have those troublesome doubts cleared up. Felipe was Spanish, just as he'd claimed. There was no question about it, now that don Gonzalo had investigated. Don Gonzalo knew the Moors as he knew his fellow Spaniards—he'd have detected it at once if Felipe had been lying.

Pedro felt a surge of eagerness. He must visit Felipe just as soon as he was allowed. The man had a story to tell, and Pedro was avidly curious to hear it.

But the next day word reached the camp which drove the

thought of Felipe from his mind. Pedro was on clean-up detail when he heard the news. He and some other young recruits—seasoned soldiers don't get assigned to clean-up details—were busy with brooms and baskets, sweeping barracks and streets and carrying away the refuse. The youths sweated as they worked, for it was late May now and the warmth of spring was deepening into summer heat. Pedro was wielding his broom with something less than vigor, wishing for a breeze, when an excited voice reached his ears.

"*Muchachos!* What do you think I just heard?" The speaker had come up on the run, a broom in his hand and excitement in his face. The sweepers stopped working and looked at him expectantly. He caught a hasty breath. "Who do you think is coming? Doña Isabella, that's who! The Queen! I was sweeping up over by the officers' tents and heard them talking. A courier brought the word not an hour ago—doña Isabella is coming to live here in the camp. She and her whole court. Imagine! The Queen, right here in—"

"Yes, yes, we heard you," someone broke in impatiently. "It's nothing to get excited about. Doña Isabella always stays at camp during a siege—didn't you know that?"

"Of course I knew it, but is that any reason I shouldn't get excited?"

Quips and comments started flying.

"Just think! We'll have the Queen herself as a neighbor."

"Hah! I doubt if we'll be exchanging any neighborly calls."

"What I can't see is, why should a queen live in a camp?"

"Oh, it's supposed to bolster the army's spirits."

"My spirits *need* bolstering, I'll say that much. Drill and work. Work and drill. It's getting monotonous."

The sweepers resumed their task, still chattering. But Pedro said not a word. He moved as if in a dream—an exciting dream, for his face was alight with eagerness. It wasn't long before his manner began drawing puzzled glances, and then a blunt question.

"What's wrong with you, Pedro?"

"Huh?" Pedro looked at the questioner vaguely. "Who, me?"

"You're the only Pedro here, aren't you? What's the matter? Why that silly smirk on your face?"

Pedro came to himself. He raked a tassel of hair back from his eyes and grinned sheepishly. "Why, the Queen's coming. Isn't that reason enough?"

But Pedro's absorption was due to something much more important to him than the Queen's impending arrival. It wasn't doña Isabella he looked forward to seeing—it was his idol, Columbus.

Since that long-ago day when the tall Genoese first appeared at La Rábida, Pedro had come to know him well. This was mainly due to Columbus's small son. Diego had been left in the friars' care while his father sought backing for his project, and Fray Juan had appointed Pedro to help the child become accustomed to his new surroundings. Pedro, being four years older than Diego, hadn't especially welcomed the assignment, but he had quickly acquired a big-brotherly fondness for his small charge, and Diego responded with warm affection.

Their friendship had brought Pedro into close touch with Columbus—Diego had seen to that—and both boys were with the man constantly during his periodic visits to La Rábida. Pedro could still recapture the thrill he had felt when he walked in the monastery garden with his two friends, father and son. He could still feel the warmth which had suffused his heart when Columbus smiled down at him. Never having known his own parents, he could almost envy Diego this wonderful father with the look of far horizons in his eyes.

Columbus was soft-spoken and often seemed remote, but when he mentioned the Enterprise—it was thus he always referred to his project—he was suddenly transformed. His voice would quicken, his face flame with ardor and take on a light that was almost mystical. Diego was too young to understand much of what his father said, and Pedro grasped only a part of it, but both listened spellbound to every word.

The Enterprise! It became a watchword with the two boys. They talked of little else when they were by themselves— Diego had learned to chatter in Spanish freely and noisily— and waited with eager confidence for the launching of the venture.

They were still waiting, Pedro reflected, though six long years had passed. But perhaps at last the wait was nearly over. Doña Isabella had shown interest in the project. But with this war going on, other things had to wait. Well, the war was drawing to an end now, or so at least it seemed.

Pedro hoped—indeed, he was almost confident—that Columbus would be with the royal party when it arrived, for he came to court often to seek support for the Enterprise. So it was no wonder that Pedro was excited. Of course, he reminded himself, seeing doña Isabella would be an honor, something he could remember with pride all his life. But there are some people even more important than queens.

The imminent arrival of the Queen caused such a furor of sweeping and scrubbing and sprucing that one got dizzy watching it. "*Madre mia!*" Paco exclaimed. "Even the dust is getting polished."

The hub of the activity was an area near the center of the camp, already partially occupied by the King's marquee and the tents of his personal retinue. Now, in the remaining space, quarters were being prepared for the Queen and the personnel of the court. Most of the young recruits managed to steal time from their work to watch the operations from a discreet distance. And it was something to see. The Queen's pavilion was a veritable palace of canvas, all vivid color and streaming pennons and gold tassels. Pedro gaped incredulously at the exquisite furniture and carpets and tapestries being taken into the tent, and the silken hangings which would partition it into separate rooms.

"It's magnificent!" he exclaimed in an awed voice.

"Fit for a queen!" Paco agreed.

Even the unimpressionable Chico blinked at the sight of such splendor.

Preparations were finished in a final flurry on the day before the Queen was to arrive. The camp got still another sweep-out, every square inch of it. The men bathed in the river and washed their work-stained clothes. Then the unit barber set up his camp-stool in the middle of the street and did a brisk business, for everybody intended to watch the

Queen's arrival, and naturally a man wants to look his best when he sees a queen, even if she doesn't see him.

Pedro, waiting his turn in the line of customers, fingered his upper lip hopefully, but couldn't feel even a hint of sprouting fuzz. He'd have to settle for just a haircut, though most of the others were getting their usual bi-weekly shave. It didn't seem fair, for the same monthly stipend was collected from every man in the unit to pay the barber for his services.

The other men on line talked as they waited. Pedro kept quiet and listened.

"I've seen many a siege and many a battle," a grizzled veteran said. "Sometimes our situation looked pretty bad. But somehow things always started looking up as soon as doña Isabella came to camp."

A scornful voice responded. "That wasn't always the case when she visited a city. What about the way she dispensed 'justice' at Seville? *Caramba!* She had people fleeing the place by the hundreds. I know—I was one of them. When a queen's own subjects flee their homes to get away from her, there's—"

"Quiet, *amigo!* Don't you know it isn't wise to question a queen's justice? Not in public, at any rate."

Someone else spoke, slowly and earnestly. "I know nothing of what doña Isabella did at Seville, but I saw her weep for pity at Moclín. Three years I spent in a Moorish dungeon there. Look at these scars!" The speaker raised both hands, showing white-scarred wrists, still disfigured and swollen from long wearing of iron gyves. "Hundreds of captives were there, chained, half-starved. We'd be there yet if the city

hadn't fallen. The Queen burst into tears as she watched our
chains struck off." The man sounded close to tears himself.
"She *wept*, mind you. Doña Isabella is more than a queen.
She is a woman, and a tender-hearted one."

Strange, Pedro thought, how what was black to one man
was white to another. Everybody seemed to have a different
image of the Queen. He wondered which came closest to the
true Isabella.

The waiting line shortened rapidly. Presently it was Pedro's turn, and for a little while the scissors click-clicked
cheerfully about his ears. The barber, unlike most of his
kind, wasn't a talkative man. He said not a word until the
job was finished. Then he gave Pedro's shoulder a friendly
tap of dismissal.

"You're all set for tomorrow, son. It's going to be a day
you'll remember."

Pedro grinned as he got up and pulled his stocking-cap
back on. The barber didn't know how truly he spoke.

The Queen Arrives

The distant cavalcade was a glittering ribbon, ablaze with color and sparkle. The sun struck fire from burnished armor, flashed a million star-points on halberd spikes, rippled flame-like on waving plumes and pennons. Pedro, standing between Paco and Chico in their usual stairstep order, watched from a little hump of land not far out from the camp. He clutched Chico's arm excitedly.

"Look at it, Chico! It's like—like a jeweled river!"

Chico considered the comparison. "I never knew a river to raise so much dust," he commented matter-of-factly. Not even the arrival of the Queen could stir *him* to any show of excitement.

Pedro's faint sigh and fainter grin reflected his mixed feelings. He was never quite sure whether Chico's perpetual calm was irritating or amusing. However, his own excitement remained undamped. He shifted restlessly from one foot to the other as he watched the slowly advancing procession. Paco seemed amused at his fidgeting.

"You won't hurry them up by wearing out your shoes," he said.

Pedro ignored the remark. "We could meet them sooner if we'd go farther along the road," he suggested.

Paco shook his head. "We're better off where we are. Not

as close as we might be, but we can see over everybody else's
head."

Glancing at the crowd on either side of the road, Pedro
agreed. Chico too nodded agreement. It was he who had
spied the little rise and pointed out its possibilities as a re-
viewing stand. Anyone as short as Chico had to keep alert for
such vantage spots.

The cavalcade was too far away to see anything but glitter,
and presently Pedro's eyes shifted back toward the camp,
where the varicolored tents and banners lent a carnival air to
an otherwise martial picture. Then he looked past the camp
to Granada's towers. There too, he knew, eyes were watching
the approaching column, and the watchers knew well what it
meant. What anger they must feel against this Queen who
dared set up her court in the very shadow of their city!

Soldiers were streaming from the camp, hurrying out to
meet the Queen. They laughed and shouted like schoolboys
on holiday as they scuffled for places among their comrades
who already lined the road. A few weeks ago that road had
been a mere mule path straggling across the vega. Now it was
broad, and packed to hardness by countless footfalls and
hoofbeats. Normally the road was busy with couriers and
supply trains coming and going, but today it was clear, ex-
tending like a long tawny carpet to meet the royal party.

Again Pedro turned toward the procession. He was still
fidgeting with impatience. "Ay! They're slower than crippled
snails!"

Paco looked at him quizzically. "Calm down, Pedro.
You're dancing around like a puppy with fleas."

"So? Isn't everybody?" Pedro kept his eyes on the cavalcade, but he knew that Paco was still watching him, so he
tried to seem nonchalant.

The minutes crawled past. The cavalcade crawled closer—
oh, so slowly. . . .

Pedro felt a touch on his arm. Chico was pointing back
toward the camp.

"Don Ferdinand," Chico announced, as casually as if he
were commenting on the weather.

"Don Ferdinand!" Pedro repeated the words uncon-
sciously, but far less casually.

Twice before Pedro had glimpsed the King from a distance,
but now he could watch him more closely as he rode from
the camp to meet the Queen, accompanied by a party of
attendants. Superbly mounted and richly dressed, he cut a
fine figure. But Pedro felt a vague sense of disillusionment.
On an ordinary horse and in ordinary clothes, don Ferdinand
would have looked a quite ordinary person. Even so, he *was*
the King, and Pedro reminded himself proudly that not
everyone was privileged to see him in the flesh.

Suddenly a deafening blast sounded from the camp. The
startled trio nearly leaped off the hillock before they realized
that it was a salvo of artillery roaring a welcome to the
Queen.

"*Caray!*" Pedro exclaimed. "For a moment I thought it
was the start of a battle."

Paco laughed, a bit shakily. "*I* thought it was the end of
the world."

A second blast roared, and a third, while drums rolled and

trumpets sounded fanfares. And then the martial music was
drowned in a mighty surge of shouting.

"*Viva doña Isabella! Viva doña Isabella!*"

The Queen's train was at hand, and the storm of cheering
that greeted it might have been heard in Granada itself.
Pedro scarcely noticed the honor guard of armored horsemen
which led the procession. He was looking beyond them, and
a thrill ran through him as for the first time in his life he saw
the Queen, Isabella of Castile.

She was a strikingly handsome woman. Somehow Pedro
had known she would be. There was high color in her face
from the brisk breeze; a sweep of auburn-gold hair, glossy as
burnished copper in the sunlight, showed under her netted
coif and wide black hat. A silver cross gleamed at her throat;
her scarlet cloak took on richer color against the black of her
bodice and skirt.

The Queen was riding a chestnut mule, whose harness was
of red leather edged with silver. She showed no sign of weariness, though the journey from Alcalá la Real must have been
tiring, and was acknowledging the soldiers' cheers with gracious smiles. With her were the young Prince Juan and the
Princesses Juana, María, and Catalina.

The honor guard divided and formed ranks on either side
of the road. The royal family dismounted. Don Ferdinand
embraced and kissed the Queen, then each of his children in
turn, and for a brief moment Pedro saw them not as unap-
proachable royalty, but as an intimate little family. Then
they remounted and rode on toward the camp together.

The cheering still continued, and it was whole-hearted and
spontaneous. True, there were those who had no great liking

for the Queen—Pedro remembered the occasional barbed comments he'd heard during the past few days—but there was only admiration in this tumultuous clamor.

"*Viva doña Isabella! Viva doña Isabella!*"

Now and then someone would dutifully yell out a "*Viva don Ferdinand!*" but it was noticeably less enthusiastic. Pedro wondered if the King resented his wife's popularity, so much greater than his own.

The royal family moved on past. The retinue which followed was a spectacle such as Pedro could never have imagined —and Pedro had a very vivid imagination. Lords and ladies paraded past on gorgeously caparisoned mounts. There were silks and brocades and laces, the sparkle of jewelry and the ripple of plumes. Pedro caught his breath at the display of courtly splendor.

But his eyes continually searched farther back along the procession—the man he was looking for wouldn't be found among these strutting peacocks.

Now the lesser lights of the court appeared—minor nobles, magistrates, priests, pages, officials of varying rank. Pedro looked at each in turn, eagerly at first, then with steadily dwindling hope. Columbus wasn't among them. Pedro's heart was a lump of lead as he watched the company move on into the camp. But the procession wasn't yet ended. He heard Paco's chuckle beside him.

"So much for the spangles. Here come the fellows who keep them polished."

Numb with disappointment, Pedro looked on apathetically, though this last section of the train was interesting in its way. There were no fewer than forty mules laden with

baggage. And what a multitude of people!—grooms and sad-
dlers, cooks and butchers, maids and laundresses, barbers,
seamstresses, shoemakers, valets—all the many, many serving
people needed to make the court a self-contained organization.

All seemed in a gay mood, peering ahead eagerly toward
the colorful encampment which was to be their home for an
indefinite period. It was a vagabond establishment, this court
of Ferdinand and Isabella, seldom in one place for long at a
time. People said waggishly that the Sovereigns spent more
time in the saddle than on the throne. The King divided his
time between the council table and the battlefield. The
Queen was everywhere; the kingdom's affairs took her from
province to province, castle to castle, camp to camp. And
where the Queen went, there went her court.

The last of the cavalcade moved in among the tents. The
soldiers began to follow in chattering groups.

"The show's over," Paco commented gaily. "Now to get
on with the war."

But Pedro found it hard to feign cheerfulness as the three
started back toward the camp. The excitement of an hour
ago had gone stale. His hopes hadn't really been warranted,
he supposed—it was only wishing that had made him so confident.

Paco's voice broke into his musing. "What on earth's the
matter, Pedro? Why so glum?"

Pedro was suddenly aware that his friend was eying him
sharply. "Oh, nothing much." He tried to grin the disappointment out of his face. "It's just that. . . ."

"It's just that he didn't show up. Is that it?"

"Didn't show up? Who?"

"Whoever it was you were looking for. You *were* looking for someone—it was written all over you."

Pedro wished that he weren't so transparent, or that Paco weren't so perceptive. He felt instinctively that the less said about Columbus, the better. But there was no point in denying what Paco so clearly guessed. "Yes. I'd rather expected to see a friend of mine. Captain Columbus."

"Captain? He's in the army?"

"No, he's a sea captain—or used to be. He hasn't been to sea now for several years. He's with the court a great deal of the time. You see, he's trying to interest the King and Queen in a project."

Paco's eyebrows shot up. "Hm-m. Your sailor friend moves in high places. How do you happen to know him?"

"Oh, he comes to La Rábida sometimes to visit Diego. Diego's his son, and he and I are good friends, so naturally I've become well acquainted with Captain Columbus. You see. . . ." And, almost without realizing it, Pedro began telling his two friends about the Enterprise.

He should have known better. He was aware how few there were who could understand that shining dream. But his own enthusiasm betrayed him. His words were eager at first, then suddenly began to falter as he saw the look that was gathering in Paco's face.

"Pedro! What kind of nonsense has that man filled your head with? Why, he must be. . . ." Words failed Paco momentarily. "You mean he actually expects to reach the east

by heading west? Vaya, fellow! Would you turn right if you
wanted to head left? Surely you don't really believe such
twaddle!"

Pedro was stung to indignation. "Of course I believe it,
and it isn't twaddle. It's entirely reasonable, the world being
round. And—"

"So the world is round, is it? And we're all balancing on a
great big ball! Pedro, Pedro, has that man got you be-
witched?" Paco shook his head almost pityingly. "I never
heard the like of that in all my life!"

"There's probably a lot you've never heard the like of,"
Pedro flared. Then with an effort he swallowed his resentment and tried to explain. "It's like this, Paco—it takes a lot
of money to get a project like the Enterprise moving. As for
the world being round, that isn't the question at all. No one
doubts that nowadays—"

"I doubt it."

"Oh, I mean no educated person doubts it." Pedro might
have been a bit more tactful.

Paco bridled. "I don't claim to be educated, but I've got
more sense than to believe that kind of foolishness."

"Oh, don't you see, Paco. . . ."

But Pedro let the words hang. He suddenly realized something of what Columbus had faced during his long struggle
to win support. He had met opposition on every hand, sneers
and mockery from the ignorant, cautious coldness from the
more intelligent. A lesser man would have given up in discouragement long ago.

It wasn't that anyone had to be convinced that the earth

is a globe—no man of learning doubted that point. Those with whom Columbus pleaded his cause admitted that his project was possible, at least in theory. But was it practical? And would it be profitable? It was a risky venture, said some. It was a dreamer's folly, said others.

Pedro shook his head hopelessly. He shouldn't have even mentioned the subject. He could never make anyone like Paco understand.

Paco was watching him, expressions of irritation and scorn and incomprehension chasing one another across his face. Suddenly his manner changed and he laid a comradely hand on Pedro's shoulder.

"Look, Pedro—suppose you don't say anything about this to anyone else. They—they mightn't understand. They'd think—well, frankly, they'd think you're not very bright." Paco looked as if he rather inclined to that opinion himself. "So if I were you, I wouldn't talk to anyone about that man Columbus and his ideas."

He spoke wheedlingly, as one might speak to a difficult child, and Pedro had to smile. Paco was right. Most of their comrades would consider such ideas a sure sign of lunacy.

"All right, Paco," Pedro agreed. "I'll say no more about it."

Chico had listened to the exchange in silence, his expressionless face turned now to one, now to the other. He hadn't seemed at all surprised at the idea of the world being round. Chico wouldn't have been surprised if he learned that the world is conical.

"And now," Paco said, his cheerful manner returning,

"let's enjoy our holiday and forget about that man Columbus."

Pedro smiled again, but the smile was forced. He was in no mood to enjoy the holiday. And he certainly wouldn't forget about that man Columbus.

Felipe

The next day doña Isabella accompanied don Ferdinand on a tour of the camp and an inspection of the troops. She was mounted on a magnificent war horse instead of the gently-stepping mule she had ridden to the camp, and like the King was in full armor. The panoply would have looked incongruous on another woman, but doña Isabella wore it with accustomed grace like the warrior-queen she was.

For the rest of the day the men were at liberty, and Pedro, somewhat recovered from his disappointment by now, seized the chance to make another visit to the hospital. The orderly on duty, the same man Pedro had talked with before, grinned in recognition and jerked a thumb toward Felipe's cot without even waiting for an inquiry.

"Yes, you can see him for a few minutes. Maybe a friendly visit is just what he needs. But you can't stay long—he's had a close call and he's still far from well."

The truth of the statement was plain in Felipe's appearance. His face was drawn, the dark skin looking even darker against the white of bandages and sheets. There was a copious stubble on his formerly smooth-shaven cheeks, so that the little tuft of beard on his chin was lost, like a small bush in a tangle of shrubbery. The man's eyes lighted at the sight of Pedro.

"Ah, my rescuer. *Ahala wsahala!*"

Pedro was momentarily disconcerted by the Arabic words, which he assumed to be a greeting. Felipe started to extend his right hand, then winced and substituted his left. "I keep forgetting. This shoulder rebels when I move my right arm. It's awkward, having to depend on my left."

Pedro clasped the extended hand warmly. Sinking down on the unoccupied adjoining cot, he glanced around at the handful of patients in the tent. "You seem to have the place pretty much to yourself," he observed, striving for the pleasantly bright tone one uses with sick people.

"Yes. Most of the others are back on duty now, thanks to the surgeons' careful attention—or perhaps in spite of it." A faint smile showed briefly, then was gone. "I've been hoping you'd stop by, Pedro. I haven't yet had a chance to thank you for saving my life—not that thanks can be adequate."

Pedro shrugged off the remark. "It was just a lucky chance that brought me there. If it hadn't been for a stray heifer. . . ." He raised his brows expressively and grinned.

"Perhaps I should thank the heifer." Again the faint smile glimmered, then faded. "So that's how you came upon me. *Allah y' fazak!*"

Pedro shot him a startled look. Arabic again!

Felipe evidently caught the look, for his expression changed subtly and he made an apologetic gesture. "Don't mind my choice of words, Pedro. You see, I've been among the Moors so long that I even think in their language. But it's a blessed relief to be using Spanish again—though I've all but forgotten how."

"You were held captive a long time, then?"

Felipe nodded slowly. "A long time, yes. Ten years."

"*Ten years!*"

"Ever since the fall of Zahara. That's where I was captured."

Pedro felt a quick surge of compassion. Zahara! He had heard the story often when the older soldiers reminisced—how, on a dark midwinter night, during the howl and roar of a fierce storm, the Moors had scaled the walls of Zahara and fallen upon the unsuspecting inhabitants. Every man, woman, and child who escaped death was taken captive to Granada, and few had ever returned.

Felipe spoke again. "Ten years! A long time, Pedro. A long, long time. . . ." His voice trailed off, and for a moment his manner seemed remote. Then he gave a little shake of his head, as if to dispel somber memories. "You were just a little fellow then, eh, Pedro?"

"Just five. Too young to understand what it was all about. But I've been told often about the attack on Zahara." Swiftly he scanned the other's face. Though it was drawn by his recent ordeal, it was clear-skinned and unlined. "You must have been quite young too when it happened."

"I was fourteen. It was fortunate I was no older—I'd doubtless have been sent to the mines. As it was, I was sold to a wealthy merchant, and he put me to work in his storehouse. It could have been worse—far worse. But I was still a captive." He had been speaking soberly, but suddenly his tone lightened and a rueful little smile played on his lips. "And look at me now—stuck like glue to this cot. I merely traded one type of captivity for another. It was the devil's own luck that put me in the way of that arquebus ball."

Pedro leaned forward, eager for more details. "They tell me it was from a Spanish arquebus. How did it happen?"

"During one of those mountain skirmishes. I was with the Moorish troops when they locked horns with the Spaniards."

"The Moorish troops! And you were with them?"

"Only long enough to get out of Granada. You see, Boabdil had called for every able-bodied man to rally to the city's defence, and civilians by the hundreds were being furnished with weapons, so as to reinforce the army in case the city was attacked. Some of the more daring fell in with the cavalry units which were being sent out against the Spaniards in the mountains. That was my chance. I helped myself to one of my master's horses and fell in with the others. It was simple enough in all that confusion. Nobody bothered to make a check—not with an enemy army just outside the walls."

"It must have been a risk, though."

"A risk well worth taking. I hadn't been in a saddle for years, but that's a skill that stays with one. I managed to separate from the others during the skirmishing, but I was scarcely clear before I was hit—by my own countrymen!" Again that smile glimmered. For a moment Felipe plucked absently at his stubble of beard. Then he went on. "Things aren't very clear after that. I remember falling from the horse, and that's about all. But I had enough of my senses left to know I had to get to the Spanish camp. Well, I tried. Most of the time I was just barely conscious. When I heard those cattle I managed to get to my feet, but couldn't find the strength to take a step. And then"—the smile flashed

suddenly broad and cheerful—"you showed up. *Allah y'*
fazak! I nearly fainted from sheer joy."

Pedro disregarded the Arabic interjection. He grinned. "*I*
nearly fainted from sheer fright."

Again Felipe's fingers stroked his unshaven cheek. Pedro
noted the gesture vaguely, a faint puzzlement stirring in his
mind, but before it could take clearer shape Felipe spoke
again. "I've been doing all the talking, Pedro. Isn't it your
turn now? What's *your* story?"

"Why. . . ." Pedro smiled and scratched his head. "I
really don't have a story." But he sketched something of his
background, rather perfunctorily, for there was much more
he wanted to learn about Felipe's. But as he tried to steer the
talk back in that direction the orderly came and decreed that
the visit was over.

"You can stay longer next time," he told Pedro, "but now
the patient needs rest."

"My jailor!" Felipe exclaimed, motioning with mock an-
noyance toward the orderly. "Just as I told you, Pedro, I'm
still a captive." A wistful note suddenly tinged his voice.
"You'll come again, won't you?"

"Of course. As often as I can," Pedro promised, then
added jokingly, "Until your jailor lets you out."

The orderly grinned. "His jailor will be only too happy to
get rid of him, the moment he can leave on his own two feet.
But we don't like to carry the patients out—it gives the
hospital a bad name."

Pedro was thoughtful as he walked back toward The Nest.
His curiosity about Felipe had been partly satisfied, but there

were still many blank spaces. He wondered if Felipe would
return to Zahara when he recovered. It would be a sad home-
coming, surely, with family, friends, and neighbors gone. The
Spanish had retaken Zahara a few years ago, but only a
military garrison lived there now. Pedro shook his head
pityingly. Evidently Felipe was utterly alone in the world.

What he had learned about the man only whetted his
desire to learn more, especially about those ten years of
captivity. Ten years! One would think that in so long a time
he'd have managed to flee the city somehow. But doubtless
he'd been closely watched. Perhaps, Pedro mused, when they
got to know each other better he might ask Felipe about
that.

His mind went back over their talk, marshaling the impressions he had gathered. Felipe struck him as a likeable
person. He seemed intelligent and well bred. That stubble of
beard gave him a somewhat uncouth appearance, though. At
the last thought, Pedro recalled Felipe's way of absently
fingering his beard, and the vague puzzlement which the gesture had evoked in him.

Suddenly he realized what had caused that curious reaction. It was Felipe's hands. Surely they weren't a laborer's
hands. They were capable but not powerful, with slender,
sensitive fingers such as might belong to a scholar rather than
to a worker in a warehouse. And, even allowing for his
present emaciated state, Felipe didn't look at all muscular.
His normal build would be slim and trim, but far from
brawny—not that of a man who has spent years handling
bales and crates of merchandise.

Of course, Pedro reflected, maybe his work had been of a

lighter nature. That was something else he might ask Felipe about when they got better acquainted. That, and a number of other things.

Young Moorish nobles still rode out from Granada at intervals to challenge Spanish knights to combat. This became an almost daily occurrence after the Queen's arrival, as if the Moors had to vent their resentment somehow, if only in such futile gestures. When their challenges were ignored, they hurled taunts at the besieging army. Proud Spanish blood seethed, but the knights stayed in the camp, restrained by don Ferdinand's order.

The Moors became ever more daring. They began to harass the borders of the camp, making sudden lunges to throw their light lances, then quickly retreating out of range of the Spaniards' weapons.

Marcos treated the attacks almost with indifference. "They relieve the monotony," he said, with the grim humor of a hardened campaigner.

"They've wounded some of our men," Pedro pointed out.

"No more than a half dozen. Not enough to matter."

"It matters to that half dozen," Pedro said dryly.

Marcos lifted his massive shoulders in a philosophic shrug. "War is war. Some get wounded. Some get killed. Some come through with a whole hide. That's the way it has to be."

It struck Pedro that Marcos, after so many years of fighting Moors, must have caught something of the Moslem's fatalism.

Once the excitement of the Queen's arrival had died down, the camp quickly settled back into its former routine.

But for Pedro there was an important difference: he now saw
Felipe almost daily. It took some planning, but he found
that a brief visit could be fitted in after arms practice, and
began stopping at the hospital each morning, coming straight
from the drill field, pike and all.

Felipe obviously welcomed the visits, and a mutual liking
sprang up, notwithstanding the gap in their ages. The man
was lonely, Pedro thought, noticing how Felipe's face brightened when he appeared and grew wistful when he left. It
made Pedro feel a little ashamed, knowing that his main motive for coming was curiosity. Felipe's pleasure in his company
was understandable—a hospital isn't the most cheerful place
in the world, even if one has comrades. And Felipe had none.
He apparently found little companionship among the handful of other patients. They weren't unfriendly, but their
interests were soldiers' interests, and their talk soldiers' talk.
Perhaps they still had some lingering suspicion of Felipe. In
any case, he was an outsider.

Pedro suspected that Felipe himself was partly responsible
for the other patients' lack of warmth. The man seemed
friendly by nature, but one often sensed a guarded reserve in
interests were soldiers' interests, and their talk soldiers' talk.
about himself. He scarcely mentioned his early life in Zahara,
and touched upon his years in Granada only when prodded.

"There's not much to tell," he said on one occasion, when
Pedro ventured to question him directly. "After I started
working in that warehouse, my life was quite ordinary." He
was absently fingering his stubbled cheek, as he had a habit
of doing.

Looking at his hands, Pedro's earlier puzzlement stirred again. "Wasn't it heavy work? Most warehouse workers are pretty husky fellows." It was a blunt remark, but tact had never been Pedro's strong point.

Felipe threw him a quick glance. Then a faint smile showed through the dark stubble. "I'm stronger than I look, Pedro. Remember, I'm not at my best just now. The fact is, however, my work didn't call for brawn. My job was to check shipments, and keep records and accounts. It happens I can write a fair hand, and I'm quick at figures."

Pedro was surprised. In that time and country, it wasn't everyone who could read and write. Perhaps Felipe sensed his surprise, for he added an explanation. "My father saw to it that I had a passable education." It was the first time he had ever mentioned any of his family, and Pedro leaned forward with heightened interest.

Felipe was silent for a moment, as if he intended to add nothing more, but to Pedro's relief he went on. "My father was a small tradesman, gradually building up his business to something more substantial. He was training me to carry on the work, so I knew Arabic fairly well even before I was taken to Granada." Pedro nodded in understanding. A merchant in the border towns, Moorish or Spanish, needed some acquaintance with both languages. Business and commerce knew no frontiers.

Felipe continued. "That's why I was brought to the warehouse in the first place—merchants are always on the lookout for clerks who can keep records in both languages. And of course the summer campaigns didn't interfere much with business—Granada's trade lines stayed open right up to the start of this siege."

"Did you have to work hard?" Pedro asked.

"Of course. Doesn't everybody? But there were slack periods, and when we weren't busy I could come and go pretty much as I pleased. I'd have been contented, after a fashion, if I'd only been free."

"Didn't you ever make plans to escape?"

"Only when I was awake," Felipe said with a flash of humor. "I could have slipped out of the city easily enough, but I'd have been recaptured within hours, with very unpleasant consequences. Granada wasn't an isolated city then, remember—it was in the heart of Moorish territory. It's quite different now, with a Spanish camp just outside the walls and all the surrounding country in Spanish hands. I lost no time in taking advantage of the changed situation."

Felipe added little to that sketchy account. At first Pedro tried to draw him out further, but then realized that he must respect the man's reticence. Perhaps his memories were too painful for casual discussion. But then, Felipe wasn't reticent only about his past, but even about his plans for the future. That, it seemed to Pedro, was being a bit *too* sensitive.

If Felipe was reserved about his own history, he showed a friendly interest in Pedro's. Pedro told him of his life at La Rábida, of Fray Juan and the other friars, of the boys who lived or studied at the monastery. He spoke cautiously when he mentioned Diego, and carefully avoided any reference to Columbus and the Enterprise. Paco's reaction to that subject was still fresh in his mind.

Felipe was gaining strength rapidly. With each visit, Pedro found him looking more fit. And with each visit he found himself enjoying the man's company more. Though Felipe skirted any details of his personal experiences, he was full of interesting bits of information about Moorish life and customs. Surprisingly, he seemed to bear no ill will toward his former masters. Once Pedro made a hesitant remark about that.

"How can you be so tolerant toward the Moors, after . . . ." He stopped, realizing that he was touching a delicate subject, but Felipe understood. For a moment he seemed to withdraw into himself, but brightened almost at once.

"Maybe if my captivity had been less tolerable, I'd be less tolerant. If, for instance, I'd spent those ten years in a dungeon, or laboring in a mine, as happens to most captives. But I was luckier than most. I suppose I see the Moors from a friendlier viewpoint."

Pedro considered this, still puzzled. Felipe hitched himself up on an elbow and watched him quizzically.

"Slaves don't *always* hate their masters, Pedro. I knew some Spanish captives in Granada who wouldn't have left if they'd had the chance. Some found their condition far better than it had been in their own country. There have been those who reached high stations, and became wealthy. Why, they might even marry into royalty—like Zoraya." Zoraya— "The Morning Star"—was the Moslem name of a captured Spanish girl who had become the power behind the Moorish throne during the reign of Boabdil's father. The story was known throughout Spain.

"Yes, I was treated decently," Felipe said. "Doubtless I'd hate Moors like vipers if I'd been starved, or beaten, or chained to a galley oar."

Pedro nodded thoughtfully. "There's no worse fate than to be a Spanish slave on a Moorish galley."

"Unless it's being a Moorish slave on a Spanish galley," Felipe retorted, with a sudden quirk on his lips.

That, Pedro reflected later, was possibly true. But it certainly wasn't the sort of remark one would expect from a Spaniard.

"For the Queen, from Tarfe!"

"*Ah-h—guah-h-h! Ah-h—guah-h-h!*"

It was one the camp waterboys, shrilly hawking his stock in trade. He wasn't more than twelve or so, but he had strong lungs, and used them to full effect as he led his burro through the teeming streets of the camp. Slung on either side of the burro were stone jugs of water, freshly drawn from the river, which the boy dispensed from a hollow cow horn to occasional customers. Besides the water, his stock included miscellaneous items likely to be needed by soldiers.

"*Ah-h—guah-h-h*—clear and cold! A copper piece buys all you can hold!"

"*Madre mia*—the lad's a poet!" Paco exclaimed. "But now that he reminds me—I'm thirsty."

"Me too," Pedro said.

Chico considered, then concurred with a nod. Whereupon all three reached for the leather water-flasks they carried at their belts. The flasks' contents was warm and stale, with a somewhat leathery taste, but it didn't cost anything. At the sight of such miserliness, the waterboy gave the trio a look of withering scorn. The look vanished abruptly when he saw Paco fumbling in his wallet.

"*Agua?*" The boy lifted his cow horn invitingly. "*This* water is fresh."

Paco shook his head. "Got any thread?"

"Of course. It's strong, and I'll pledge there's not a snarl in a spoolful. That'll be two *blancas.* How about needles? Hosepoints? Soap?"

"Just the thread."

"Need any laundering done? I scrub clothes clean, and my fee is small."

"I never have any laundry. When my clothes get dirty, I just throw them away and buy new ones."

The boy shrugged, dropped the proceeds of his sale into his wallet, and led the burro on. "*Ah-h—guah-h-h! Ah-h—guah-h-h!*"

It was Sunday afternoon, which meant no drills, no tasks other than essential ones, and several hours of uninterrupted freedom. The trio had started on an aimless stroll, undecided how to spend the free period.

"Let's take another walk around the artillery ground," Pedro suggested.

Chico was willing, but Paco shook his head. "Too long a walk—I've got sentry duty coming up this evening. Suppose we have another look at the Queen's pavilion."

Pedro threw him an amused glance. "Who do you think you're fooling? Of course, there aren't any girls to watch at the artillery ground." He shrugged. "All right, we'll go see the Queen's pavilion—we've only seen it a dozen times."

The trio moved on, in their usual stairstep order—the tall Paco, the medium-high Pedro, and the diminutive Chico. As they drew near the canvas palace, Paco suddenly stopped and struck an attitude of mock puzzlement. "I'm sure there's a slight difference between that pavilion and The Nest. But I can't quite put my finger on what it is."

"What do you expect?" Pedro said chidingly. "Would you have the Queen live in a brushwood shelter?"

"Heaven forbid!" Paco broke into a cynical chuckle, still taking in the pavilion's splendor. "How selfless our Queen is! How bravely she shares the hardships of camp with her soldiers!" He was prudently keeping his voice to a murmur. When one speaks irreverently of queens, one speaks softly.

The three didn't dare go closer to the court precinct, but by skirting it at a respectful distance they could catch glimpses of the world of the highborn. It was a world they could never enter, nor would they wish to, but it was something to enjoy watching, though not to be taken too seriously.

Just outside the precinct a groom was exercising a Barbary steed. Pedro eyed the animal admiringly. "Beautiful, no?"

"Lovely," agreed Paco.

"Look at those sleek muscles!"

"Pretty hair, too," observed Paco.

"And that dainty, high-stepping pace!"

"Gives her skirts a saucy swish, eh?" Paco commented appreciatively.

It dawned on Pedro that there was some discrepancy in their observations. Paco had no eye for a spirited horse—not when there was a pretty girl to watch. Pedro followed his gaze and switched his own attention to the serving-maid who had emerged from one of the tents with an armload of linen. She made a pleasing picture in her white coif and neat brown

dress. Disappointingly, she went into another tent at once, so
he turned back to the Barbary steed. It struck him suddenly
that it looked slightly familiar. Chico had already recognized
it.

"It's don Gonzalo's horse—the one Boabdil gave him," he
announced, in his characteristic casual tone.

Pedro nodded. "You're right, it is. I've never seen a finer
animal." His tone became thoughtful. "I wonder how it feels
to be at war with a friend, the way don Gonzalo is with
Boabdil."

Paco gave a little sniff. "Serves him right for making
friends with a Moor."

"That's no way to talk," Pedro protested. "Don Gonzalo
is—"

He broke off, startled by sudden shouts and a rapidly
approaching thudding of hoofs. The three whirled, and saw a
mounted figure coming at full gallop along the street leading
from the camp's border. For an instant they stood rigid in
astonishment. Then they leaped aside, just in time to avoid
being run down.

Pedro stared in unbelief. The horseman was a robed and
turbaned Moor! He carried a lance, and he was barely past
Pedro when he reined in his mount, drew back his arm, and
hurled the lance with all his force into the court precinct. It
thudded quivering in the earth, only yards away from the
Queen's pavilion. With a savage yell the Moor whirled his
mount and galloped back the way he had come.

The act had been so sudden, so completely unexpected
that at first the soldiers were too startled to move. Now they
snapped into action and ran to head him off. They were too

late. The Moor's charger galloped past the sentries, topped the high-piled earthworks outside the camp, then cleared the wide trench beyond in a prodigious leap. The rider flung back a shouted taunt as he sped away in a flurry of dust. A volley of crossbow bolts, too hastily aimed to come near their target, whistled harmlessly in his wake.

In the court precinct, the occupants of the tents were hurrying out, attracted by the commotion. A knight dashed over to the lance and pulled it out of the ground, and Pedro saw that a strip of paper was tied to the shaft. The knight bent to scan the paper, and his face darkened. He raised his voice in an angry shout that carried to the men outside the precinct.

"It says: 'For the Queen!' "

There was a flurry of shocked indignation, silenced at once as the knight shouted again. "It's written in Spanish. And there's a signature: 'Tarfe.' "

"For the Queen, from Tarfe!" The inscription's insolent words passed from man to man in the swiftly gathering crowd.

"Who is this Tarfe?" men demanded of one another.

"Whoever he is, may his black heart shrivel!" someone snarled.

The Moor's mad dash into the camp grated hard on touchy Spanish pride, but it was the insult to their Queen that infuriated the men. They might have private reservations about doña Isabella, might even guardedly put them into words, but this open affront—and from a heathen Moor! —was insufferable. The crowd continued to grow as word of the outrage spread through the camp.

Pedro and his two companions lingered, sharing the crowd's angry mood, until presently Paco remembered that he must report for sentry duty. The three started back toward the barracks, but Pedro suddenly halted.

"It's still early, and the hospital's close by. I'll stop in and tell Felipe about this. Want to come along, Chico?"

Chico shook his head emphatically. "Not me. I'd rather stay away from hospitals. I'll go back to The Nest with Paco."

Pedro turned aside and moved on alone to the hospital. He found Felipe sitting up in his cot, looking almost fit again. At the sight of Pedro's grim face his welcoming smile faded to a look of questioning concern. Pedro, still burning with indignation, responded to his greeting with unintentional abruptness, then immediately started pouring out an account of what had happened. But before he got to the inscription on the lance he was interrupted by an incredulous exclamation.

"*Bismillah!* You mean to say that a single Moor rode halfway through the camp and back again!" Felipe hitched himself forward on the cot. His eyes were glowing strangely. "And no one intercepted him?"

"It happened too suddenly," Pedro protested. "Everybody was too startled to move."

"But a single Moor! Defying thousands of Spaniards!" Was it indignation that rang in Felipe's voice? It sounded almost like admiration. "What audacious, harebrained boldness!"

Pedro looked at him with surprised resentment. "You seem to think it's something to admire," he flared.

A hint of sardonic amusement touched the other's face. "Boldness is admirable, even in a Moor."

"There's nothing admirable about insulting the Queen!" Pedro flung back.

"The Queen? What about the Queen?"

"You didn't let me finish. There was a paper tied to the lance, with writing on it. 'For the Queen,' it said. You call *that* admirable?"

Felipe's face went suddenly grave. "Of course not, Pedro. That was unworthy of any soldier, Moor or Spaniard." He tugged musingly at the growth on his cheek, then asked, "Was there anything else on the paper?"

"Only a signature—'Tarfe.' "

"Tarfe! I might have known." Felipe caught Pedro's inquiring look, and explained. "Tarfe is a Granadine knight— arrogant as a lion and vain as a peacock. He's a reckless daredevil, just the sort who *would* make a spectacular dash like that. It was pure bravado, of course. And yet. . . ." He squinted pensively, then shook his head as if in wonder. "And yet, it *was* a bold exploit."

Pedro didn't answer. He was puzzled and angered by Felipe's attitude. Why, the man seemed almost to be applauding the Moor's act. Felipe evidently sensed his feelings, for he threw him an apologetic smile.

"Maybe I'm not as indignant as I should be, Pedro. Just put it down to my stay among the Moors." There was an uncomfortable silence, then Felipe made an obvious attempt to change the subject. "It's good of you to stop by. You're always welcome, you know. Time hangs heavy in a hospital."

The man's tone was so wistful that Pedro would have felt heartless not to respond. He followed Felipe's lead and dropped the subject of Tarfe. "You seem to have profited by your stay. You're looking better than I've seen you yet." Then he eyed Felipe's unshaven cheeks critically. "But I must say you'd look better yet if you'd get that beard trimmed."

"Why should I? I'm not going anywhere." Felipe laughed, seeming relieved that their little clash was settled. He gestured toward the tent walls. "Here I am—a captive in a canvas prison, with bandages for chains, still dreaming of escape. It isn't pleasant, but there's nothing I can do about it. So. . . ." He lifted his brows humorously. "*Inshallah!* So be it!"

Pedro frowned slightly. Those Arabic exclamations sprinkled so freely in Felipe's speech were disconcerting.

A little later he took leave of Felipe with his usual parting pleasantry. But as he walked back toward The Nest he was vaguely troubled, though he wasn't certain just why.

As was to be expected, the talk around the supper fires was all about Tarfe. Until today, perhaps not a man in the camp had ever heard of Tarfe; now they tossed his name about incessantly, and spoke it as if it burned their tongues. Yet there was a grudging recognition of his boldness, and it occurred to Pedro that perhaps Felipe's attitude hadn't been so unreasonable after all. The very audacity of the Moor's mad dash might have won some respect, but for his affront to the Queen. That cheapened the deed and made it contemptible.

Paco returned from his round of sentry duty shaking his head wonderingly. "I've been standing watch over by the earthworks, and I took a long look at that trench Tarfe cleared. *Madre mia!* What a jump that was! We dug those trenches ourselves—I wouldn't have thought there was a horse alive who could clear them."

Pedro raked his cap back and ran his fingers through his hair. "I didn't notice it at the time, but come to think of it, that was a splendid animal. I'm surprised Tarfe would risk hurting it. I've heard that Moors value their horses more than their wives."

"That's natural." Paco grinned. "Only a wealthy Moor can own more than one horse. But a Moor is poor indeed if he can't afford a spare wife or two."

The groups around the fires began to disperse. The men's anger had cooled now, their mood was more normal. When the six barrackmates went into The Nest, Marcos snapped his fingers resoundingly, as if he'd just thought of something.

"Tarfe, the Moor, and Pulgar, the Spaniard! Two of a kind, it strikes me." He lumbered over to his corner of the dark shelter. "I suppose you youngsters have heard about how Pulgar slipped into Granada last year?"

There was no immediate response, then Pedro spoke up. "Pulgar? What Pulgar was that?" Like the others, he'd heard the story often, but he didn't want to deny Marcos the pleasure of recounting it.

"Hernán del Pulgar, of course. 'He of the exploits,' they call him—and with reason. Talk about daring feats . . . !

Anyway, when we were in the vega last year there came a
long dull stretch, and Pulgar got bored. So, just to pass the
time, he. . . ."

Pedro listened with half an ear as he got out of his clothes.
He knew the story already—how the venturesome Pulgar,
bored with the monotony of camp life, had enlisted a dozen
or so other young daredevils and, with a renegade Moor as a
guide, slipped off one dark night toward Granada. The Moor
led them to a culvert in the wall, through which a branch of
the river flowed, nearly dry at that season. Silently the little
party had crept through the culvert and made their way into
the very heart of the dark city. There, upon the door of the
principal mosque, they posted a placard bearing the words,
"*Ave Maria.*" Men still chuckled over the episode, imagining
the Moors' chagrin when, upon discovering the placard the
following morning, they realized that their city had been
"invaded."

Marcos chuckled now as he finished the story. "*Diablos!*
I'd have given a month's pay—which I admit isn't much—
just to see those heathen faces. All the same, Pulgar and his
companions were rash young fools. They might all have been
killed—and for what?" He grunted. "Yes, Pulgar's feat and
Tarfe's were pretty much alike—all dash and splurge, but no
sensible purpose. That isn't the way wars are won."

Andrés's glum voice sounded in the darkness. "You're
right. But young Pulgar is looked on as a hero by everybody
—including himself."

"I know. He does have courage, if he'd only learn to season
it with sense. He's like don Ferdinand in that respect."
Marcos lowered his mighty voice to a mere bellow. "Our

King is also more rash than wise at times—though of course that's only what I'm thinking. I'd never dare say it aloud."

Again Marcos chuckled. It was his softest chuckle, and only slightly shook the walls.

New Confidant

"Sentry six?"

"Sentry six, sir. All's well, by God's grace."

"May He be thanked. Keep alert."

Pedro heard the prescribed exchange between the duty officer and the next sentry in the line. Then there was silence for a few minutes, save for the clop-clop of hoofs as the officer rode along the sentry line in his direction. The mounted figure loomed out of the darkness and paused beside Pedro.

"Sentry seven?"

"Sentry seven, sir. All's well, by God's grace."

"May He be thanked. Keep alert."

The shadowy form moved on and the hoofbeats receded. Pedro sighed, wishing he was in The Nest asleep, instead of out here patrolling the camp's dark borders. Sentry duty was bad enough in the daytime, but it was even worse at night, especially when you were tired all over from digging ditches. The back-breaking work was all the fault of that Moor, Tarfe—blast his heathen hide! His dash into the camp had made it plain that the defenses were inadequate, which meant that the trenches had to be widened and deepened, and the earthworks piled higher. Ay! Pedro's muscles still ached from wielding that shovel. He'd like to break it over Tarfe's head—first removing his turban. Well, the work was finished, thank the saints! Tarfe couldn't leap over that trench now—not unless his horse grew wings.

Pedro sighed again, then perked up a bit at the thought that the watch was in its last hour. Soon he'd be relieved. Now that the work was finished, he supposed the old routine would be resumed. He'd stop at the hospital and see Felipe in a day or two, after he'd caught up on lost sleep. He still couldn't make up his mind about Felipe. The man was likeable, but there was something about him that was baffling, something he couldn't quite pin down. Doubtless it was due to those long years among the Moors. *Santos!* An experience like that would leave its mark on anybody. If only he'd stop sprinkling his speech with Arabic—those foreign expressions sounded positively heathen!

It was still hot, though the sun had been gone for hours. Pedro wearily shifted his pike to the other shoulder and slapped at a bothersome mosquito. Sentry duty! It was the one thing about army life that he thoroughly hated. But he'd better get used to it—it was good training for the watches he'd have to stand when he went to sea with Captain Columbus.

The thought of Captain Columbus sent Pedro drifting off into a pleasant reverie. He was watchful, subconsciously. Any unusual sound or movement would have snapped him instantly alert. But his thoughts were elsewhere as he slowly paced his post, remembering. . . .

Remembering how he used to dream, back at La Rábida, of having a personal part in the Enterprise. From the monas-

tery, situated on a bluff by the entrance to the Rio Tinto, he
had watched vessels moving upriver toward the harbor of
Palos, only a mile and a half away, or down toward the sea,
which was even closer. Gazing seaward, his heart would fill
with longing, his imagination would come alive with pictures
of the exotic East which, Captain Columbus said, could be
reached by sailing west. If only he too might make that
westward voyage—sail to that great unknown beyond the
horizon!

Pedro remembered vividly the day he had made bold to
open his heart to his idol. It was during one of Columbus's
visits to La Rábida to see Diego. The three—Columbus,
Diego, and Pedro—had been strolling in the monastery garden, when Diego remembered a "map" he had drawn for his
father—"to guide you on your voyage," he explained. The
little fellow had hurried off to fetch his childish creation,
leaving Pedro alone with Columbus. It was a chance he'd
been waiting for. Pedro seized it quickly, lest he lose courage,
and blurted out his secret hope. Columbus had smiled down
at him—that smile which adults reserve for children's impractical ideas.

"Don't you think you're a bit young to go sailing off on
voyages?"

"I'm nearly eleven, sir, and I know a lot about ships—I
spend all my holidays down at the harbor—and Captain
Pinzón has shown me all about tackle and rigging and such
things—and I've gone sailing with the Pinzón boys and can
handle a boat as well as they can—or almost, anyway, and—"
Pedro's list of qualifications was interrupted as he gasped for
breath.

Columbus had nodded approvingly. "It's a good beginning. By San Fernando! It seems you've got the sea in your blood, Pedrito. I hadn't realized that."

"Then"—Pedro was eager, beseeching—"then I *can* go with you, sir?"

"Why not? Provided, of course, that Fray Juan doesn't object."

Pedro's joy had nearly choked him. "Oh, Fray Juan won't object, sir—not if *you* say it's all right."

Diego had rejoined them then, proudly displaying his "map," and Columbus turned to give smiling approval to the crude drawing. Pedro was walking on golden clouds. He said nothing to Diego of his intention—the child would have been hurt at the thought of their being separated—nor had he mentioned it again to Columbus, for there was no chance to be alone with him. But from that day on Pedro's whole world had centered on the Enterprise.

No one had imagined then that the project would remain pending so long. Year had followed year, while Columbus worked incessantly, always on the verge of success, never quite reaching it. The man had known disappointment, discouragement, frustration at every turn. Yet his faith in his dream had never faltered. Nor had Pedro's.

During those years the boy had spent all his free time at the Palos harbor, exploring ships, clambering about rigging, absorbing nautical knowledge from sailors and dock workers. Fray Juan had noticed his love for the sea and encouraged it—Pedro wondered if he guessed its cause—so the boy was given ample opportunity to pursue his interest. By the time he turned fifteen he had learned considerable seamanship.

With Fray Juan's influence, he could have shipped out on one of the vessels which were blockading the Mediterranean coast to prevent supplies from reaching Granada from Moslem North Africa. The kindly prior had seemed surprised when Pedro elected to join the army instead, but his only comment had been a quizzical, "I thought the sea was your first love, Pedro." Perhaps he surmised the reason for Pedro's choice.

Pedro had thought the matter out carefully. Columbus, he knew, was pleading his cause with the King and Queen in castle and in camp. So, Pedro reasoned, should he ship out on a blockade vessel, the Enterprise might be launched without his knowledge while he was at sea. On the other hand, by joining the army he'd have some chance of keeping in touch with developments. Where the army was, there were the Sovereigns, and where the Sovereigns were, there Captain Columbus was likely to be, sooner or later. That had been ample reason for turning soldier rather than sailor for the duration of this campaign.

Pedro didn't regret the choice, though as yet it hadn't achieved the result he'd hoped for. He didn't know where Captain Columbus was now, but wherever he might be, he was still pursuing his dream, that was certain. And the endeavor might even yet bring him here to the camp.

Pedro paced on. Presently he heard the voices of the duty officer and the next sentry, and a few minutes later the officer's round brought him again to Pedro's post.

"Sentry seven?"

"Sentry seven, sir. All's well, by God's grace."

"May He be thanked. Keep alert."

The officer rode on toward the next station, and again Pedro was alone with his thoughts. He resumed his steady pacing, his mind still shifting back and forth between the remembered past and the dreamed-of future. To Pedro, in that moment, it seemed a very bright future indeed.

Yes, all was well, by God's grace.

The next day Pedro paid another visit to the hospital. He found Felipe sitting upright on the cot, hands clasped around his knees, a look of impatience on his face. When he saw Pedro the expression gave place to a welcoming smile.

"I was beginning to think you'd deserted me," he said lightly, yet with a touch of seriousness.

"Oh, they've been keeping us busy since Tarfe— Ah, since I saw you last." Pedro made the amendment hastily, remembering that he'd better avoid the touchy subject of Tarfe.

Felipe understood. His smile broadened briefly, then the impatient look reappeared. "That orderly must have got lost. I've been sitting here for hours—well, ten minutes, anyway —waiting for him to fetch me some clothes."

"Clothes? So you're able to get up now."

"Oh, yes. I've been up and about often here in the tent. Now I want to get out into the open, if I can lay my hands on something to wear. They tell me my own clothes were burned."

"I know—I'm the one who burned them." Pedro grinned. "You couldn't wear them anyway—not here in camp. Moorish clothes aren't very popular around here."

He studied Felipe's face, pleased to see how fit he looked.

The traces of illness were all but gone. The beard, still untrimmed, was blacker and heavier now, partly hiding the hollows under the cheekbones and making the leanness of his face less noticeable. All in all, he showed little resemblance to the haggard figure of a few weeks ago.

Felipe's eyes moved past Pedro and his face brightened. "Ah—at last! My dilatory attendant."

The orderly came up carrying some clothing over one arm and a pair of boots in his hand. "The boots are your own," he said, depositing them beside the cot. "I managed to get these other clothes from the general supplies, and it wasn't easy." He laid them on the foot of the cot. "There you are—now maybe you'll stop nagging me."

"If I didn't nag I'd never get results," Felipe said cheerfully, then added a word of thanks as the orderly moved away. He pushed the sheet aside, swung his legs over the edge of the cot, and reached for the clothing. He sat there for a moment eying the garments, as if he found them unfamiliar. Pedro watched him with faint amusement.

"*Vaya*, Felipe! Don't sit there looking at them all day— put them on."

Felipe smiled and began drawing on the hose, which were in effect skintight trousers, being joined at the top to form a single garment. His movements were awkward and uncertain, and Pedro watched him in growing surprise, wondering if his ineptness was due to his stiff shoulder.

"*Hombre!*" Pedro exclaimed in good-humored impatience. "Don't tell me you've even forgotten how to get into Spanish clothes!"

"Almost. But it'll come back to me with practice." Felipe

bent forward to pull on the calf-length, curve-toed boots. They were Moorish footgear—the same he had been wearing when Pedro first saw him.

"Smart-looking boots," Pedro commented.

"Yes. The leather's scuffed, but they're still sound and serviceable."

"They look sort of military," Pedro said, then added with puzzled bluntness. "The Moors must dress their captives well."

The remark was out before he realized its tactlessness. Felipe paused, his hands still on a boot top, and remained thus for a moment without moving. Then he sat up, and Pedro saw that his face wore a strangely remote look. But his voice was casual, even flippant, when at last he spoke.

"I see what you mean. The fact is, Pedro, I raided my master's storehouse before quitting his service. I not only 'borrowed' his horse, but his clothes as well."

Pedro felt uncomfortable about his tactless remark, but he was glad to have that matter explained. He had wondered often about those boots, and the good quality of the Moorish clothes which had shown even through the stains and tatters.

Felipe started drawing on the shirt, moving gingerly, favoring the injured shoulder. Seeing his difficulty, Pedro gave him a hand, then helped with the doublet, which was a somewhat smarter garment than his own out-dated tunic. He stepped back and looked him over approvingly.

"What a difference clothes can make! All you need now is a shave. Don't you think it's time you're getting rid of those whiskers?"

Felipe smiled and fingered his bristly cheeks. "I think I'll keep my beard. I've become rather fond of it. A beard is like some people—it grows on one." He grasped Pedro's arm eagerly. "Come along, Pedro. I want to see what the outside world looks like."

His eyes were bright with pleasure when they stepped out of the tent. He threw back his head and let the warm sunlight fall full upon his face. "Ah-h-h—sunshine! We don't appreciate it until we're denied it."

Pedro laughed. "Maybe *you* appreciate it. The rest of us are looking for shade, these days." He gestured toward the street which adjoined the hospital compound. "You can see something of the camp from over there, Felipe. Then when you're stronger you must explore the place. It's something to see."

Walking slowly, they moved to the edge of the street. Pedro swept his arm in an arc to take in the camp around them. "Quite a place, eh, Felipe?"

There was no response, and Pedro turned to Felipe questioningly. Felipe wasn't looking at the camp. He was looking along the street which cut a wide straight path to the camp's border, his gaze fixed on a point far beyond, where Granada's towers rose. His eyes burned strangely; his face was intent, wearing an expression Pedro couldn't analyze.

There was an interval of silence. Then Felipe made a slight shrugging motion, as if to shake off his absorption. "I'm afraid I was woolgathering," he said, with an apologetic little laugh. "I was thinking how different Granada looks from the outside than from within."

He looked around at the camp now, made some interested

comments, and asked a few questions. But before long his gaze again wandered toward Granada, as if drawn there irresistibly. Presently he began pointing out various features of the city, describing them as they would appear from close at hand. Pedro was fascinated by the intimate glimpse of alien Granada.

Felipe's tone grew somber when his eyes shifted from the city to the ruined vega. "It was beautiful there once, Pedro. I used to forget everything else when I'd look out at the vega, all green and rusty-brown, with little hamlets scattered here and there, and men working in the fields looking tiny as ants." There was a strange wistfulness in his face. "Now it's all gone, except for that green strip just outside the walls."

Pedro looked at the broad belt of greenery which extended along the city's borders. It was perhaps a mile in width, edged on its farther side by the massive walls, its nearer limits defined sharply where the green growth met the blackened ruin of the vega, marking the limits of the previous autumn's ravages. Looking at it, Pedro could imagine how the entire vega must once have appeared.

"What grows in that green strip, Felipe? Is it all just trees and grass, or do they grow crops there?"

"There are some orchards and vineyards and olive groves. But much of it is parkland. You know—shady groves and flower gardens. The whole place is a sort of resort for recreation in peacetime. Every Moor who can afford it—and some who can't—has a pleasure lodge there."

"Pleasure lodge?"

"Yes. A small country house where they can get away from

the city and relax. You can see some of them from here—
those towers showing here and there. Of course, they aren't
being used these days."

"I'm sure they aren't," Pedro said dryly.

A little later, Felipe reluctantly suggested that they go
back to the tent. "I'm still a bit shaky in the knees," he
admitted. "But give me another week and I'll be as good as
new. Allah y' fazak! How glad I'll be when I can leave my
canvas prison for good!"

"And then what, Felipe? What do you intend to do after
you leave?"

It was a natural question to ask, and should have been easy
to answer. But Felipe was silent for a noticeably long interval. When he did respond it was only with a slight shrug
and a noncommittal, "Who knows?"

Pedro felt a bit annoyed. Surely the man had given some
thought to his plans for the future. Did he have to be so
closemouthed? Then Pedro grinned inwardly as a sudden
thought struck him. Just look who was being critical! Wasn't
he himself just as closemouthed as Felipe, when it came to
his own plans for the future? Didn't he guard his speech
constantly, lest he let something slip about Captain Columbus and the Enterprise?

Suddenly, for no clear reason, a feeling of resentment
swept Pedro. Why should he keep quiet about the Enterprise, avoiding the subject as if it were a guilty secret? He
was certainly tired of keeping it locked inside him. He
couldn't talk about it to his comrades, knowing how they'd
scoff, but he didn't have to guard his tongue with Felipe. If

Felipe should scoff, he'd be cheapening himself, not Captain Columbus—and he, Pedro, would tell him so.

The resolve made, he carried it out with no delay. The two were scarcely back in the tent when he began talking about his life at La Rábida. Felipe looked surprised at the abrupt introduction of the subject, but showed his usual friendly interest. Pedro led up to his point gradually, alluding first to Diego, then to Columbus, and finally—with hesitance— getting around to the Enterprise. He kept watching Felipe, ready to flare up at the least sign of disrespect to his idol.

He needn't have been so touchy. Felipe didn't scoff. On the contrary, his face lighted with enthusiasm.

"It's an exciting idea, Pedro. Sounds reasonable, too. If the world is round—and men who should know say it is—then why *shouldn't* we be able to reach the Indies by sailing westward? The theory should be tested, at any rate. And this friend of yours—Columbus, you say his name is?—sounds as if he's just the man to test it."

Pedro's heart turned an elated flip-flop. Suddenly his last uneasy doubts about Felipe dissolved like wisps of smoke. Anyone who approved of Captain Columbus *had* to be all right!

From that day on, Pedro looked upon Felipe as a valued friend, in some respects closer than even his comrades in The Nest. With Felipe he could talk freely about the subject that meant so much to him. He felt as if a gag had been removed from his mouth, and made full use of this sudden new freedom. Often and at length and with eager enthusiasm he pursued the topic, and if Felipe sometimes wished he'd talk about something else, he was a good fellow and didn't say so.

But one thing Pedro still kept to himself—his dream of having a personal part in the great venture. To Pedro, that was something between Captain Columbus and himself, to be shared with no one else.

"Prepare for Action"

The long June days passed uneventfully, each as like the one
before as the repeated refrain of a song. Drill sessions filled a
part of the mornings, and caring for gear and quarters took a
bite out of the day, but there was little else that needed
doing. The problem was no longer how to find leisure time,
but how to keep it occupied. By the Queen's command,
gambling was prohibited. So was brawling. And, Marcos
complained, if a soldier couldn't amuse himself by losing his
pay at dice, or getting battered to a pulp by a comrade's fists,
what was there left?

"Things weren't like this in the old army," he growled one
evening as the men gathered around the supper fires. "No
one used to see any harm in a little gambling between
battles. And if a man lost all his money to one of his friends,
he could draw a dagger and cut out his gizzard. All in fun, of
course. Nobody objected."

"Not even the friend who lost his gizzard?" Paco asked
innocently.

Marcos ignored him. "Soldiers were soldiers in those
days. Fighting and gambling came as naturally as eating.
Diablos! We had more casualties from camp brawls than
from enemy action. But at least we didn't get bored." His

bushy brows met in a savage scowl over eyes that showed a
telltale twinkle. "And now look what the army's come to!
The only reason a man can draw a dagger is to slice his
mutton." Suiting action to word, he sliced off a slab of meat
with his blade, skewered it on the point, and bit off a massive
mouthful.

Pedro chuckled. "I suppose when you weren't busy carving
one another up, you found time to fight the enemy." But he
knew that there was a grain of truth in Marcos's exag-
gerations.

Not being addicted to either gambling or brawling, Pedro
found nothing irksome in the Queen's edict. Nor did it
bother him when she issued an order forbidding any profanity or unseemly language. That set Marcos to growling in
his beard again.

"Unseemly language! Just what kind of language does the
Queen consider unseemly? *Diabl—!*" He bit off the word
sharply and substituted a milder expletive. "*Vaya!* This is an
army camp, not a monastery. And you can stop grinning,
Pedro—it's no joke."

Day followed sultry day. June was slowly burning itself
out. Through shimmering heat waves one could see snow on
the higher mountain slopes, but the vega lay baking in the sun
like slowly browning toast. Most of the men discarded hose
and tunics, thrust bare feet into sandals of tough esparto
grass, and wore only shirt and underbreeches—it was quite
conventional for the latter to come unblushingly into the
open in hot weather. Pedro was still wearing his seaman's
stocking-cap, though otherwise as scantily clad as his comrades.

"Why wear a cap, hot as it is?" Paco demanded one afternoon. "Why not go bareheaded, or wear a kerchief, like a sensible person?"

"I never claimed to be a sensible person." Pedro grinned as he pulled the cap on over his mop of hair. It was a wet mop at the moment, for he'd just taken a cooling dip in the river with Paco and Chico. "I'm so used to this cap that I'd feel only half-dressed without it."

"You're only half-dressed anyway," Chico pointed out matter-of-factly.

Pedro grinned again, and the trio headed back toward The Nest. Pedro didn't feel called upon to explain that he couldn't bring himself to stop wearing the cap. It was the badge of a sailor, and privately he considered himself a sailor, even though he *was* in the army.

Pedro saw Felipe often. Felipe seemed quite fit now, aside from his still-bandaged arm, which he carried stiffly and had to favor considerably. He was active, though, and made himself useful about the hospital at various tasks. Understandably, he seemed averse to staying in the tent, and was often absent when Pedro came.

"I was out exploring the camp," he would explain afterward. "I saw enough of this hospital while I was flat on my back. Now that I'm upright again, I like a change of scenery now and then."

Pedro was disappointed and almost resentful on these occasions. He looked forward to his talks with Felipe, and felt cheated when he missed them. How else could he talk about Captain Columbus and the Enterprise?

July was a week old when Pedro realized suddenly that

their companionship would soon come to an end. Not that
he hadn't known it all along, but such things have a habit of
creeping up on one and springing unexpectedly. He had
come to the hospital earlier than usual one afternoon, so as
to get there before Felipe set off somewhere without him. He
found Felipe exchanging bantering remarks with one of the
orderlies.

"Who'll do your work for you when I'm gone?" he was
saying as Pedro came in. "I won't be around here much
longer, you know."

"I'll be glad to get rid of you." The orderly grinned. "If
you were in the army you'd have been back on duty long
ago."

"If I were in the army I wouldn't have been here in the
first place," Felipe retorted. Then he saw Pedro and threw
him a welcoming smile.

Pedro was hard put to return the smile. His spirits had
taken a sudden drop. Felipe would be leaving the camp for
good when he was released from the hospital. They might
never see each other again. And the time evidently was close.
Ay!

Pedro put on a cheerful expression and exchanged some
pleasantries with the other two. When Felipe suggested a
walk he assented readily, resolved to question his friend
about his plans. Felipe had been oddly evasive on that subject before, but he must have decided something by now.

Never one to waste time, Pedro brought up the question
directly as soon as the two were out of the tent. "I gather
that you'll soon be leaving, Felipe. What do you intend to do
then?"

Felipe's answer was far from informative. "Oh, I don't know. I'll think about it when the time comes."

Pedro shot him an annoyed glance. The other's offhand manner puzzled him. Felipe didn't seem the kind who'd be that thoughtless.

Perhaps Felipe sensed something of his thoughts, for after a moment he added casually, "I've got experience in merchandising. I'll find work somewhere. Anyway, I'll probably be here for a while yet." He dropped the subject as if it were unimportant. "Where to, Pedro? Any ideas?"

Pedro threw him another quick glance. Well, he told himself, it wasn't *his* problem. He needn't worry about Felipe's future—obviously Felipe didn't. He put the matter out of his mind.

"Suppose we go over to the drillfield and see if the cavalry horses are being exercised. It's a real show to watch them go through their paces."

As they moved on through the camp Pedro realized that he had to stretch his legs slightly to keep up with Felipe's springy strides. Felipe seemed full of energy, his manner pleasant and untroubled. He still carried his arm stiffly, and probably always would, but aside from that looked quite fit. No doubt about it, his stay at the hospital could be ended almost any day now.

The two were nearing the drillfield when they heard shouts and laughter up ahead. Curious, they quickened their pace. The gleeful clamor came from a crowd of soldiers lined along the edge of the field.

"What's going on?" Felipe asked.

"I think I know." Pedro, until now still a bit pensive,

perked up expectantly. "We'll never push through that crowd. Let's circle around where we'll be able to see."

They did so. When they saw what was causing the hilarity, they too burst out laughing. In front of the crowd were a man and a donkey—the man tied by the wrists to the donkey's tail. Red-faced with shame and fury, he was leaping and shouting and jerking his bound wrists in an effort to get the donkey moving, all the while keeping a wary eye on the beast's unpredictable hoofs. The donkey stood stubbornly motionless, indifferent alike to the man and the spectators.

"What's this all about?" Felipe demanded, when he was able to speak.

"He's under punishment," Pedro explained, motioning toward the unlucky captive. "He has to circle around the field tied to the donkey's tail."

An onlooker stopped laughing long enough to add further explanation. "The rogue was caught thieving from a sleeping barrackmate. That's as low as a man can get." Pedro nodded emphatic agreement, torn between indignation at the crime and amusement at its consequences. The other went on. "What he's getting is too good for him—he ought to be soundly flogged."

The fuming culprit continued his frenzied efforts to get the beast moving. The donkey, with donkey-like stubbornness, refused to cooperate. The man edged around to one side and started slapping at the beast's rump. The donkey made no move. The man tried again, pounding harder. Whereupon the beast threw him a reproachful look and suddenly started forward, nearly jerking him off his feet. For a dozen paces the animal advanced, dragging the hanger-on along, then halted so abruptly that a collision resulted. The onlookers roared, choked, and held their sides.

"My sympathy is all for the donkey," Felipe said between bursts of laughter. "After all, the poor beast didn't steal anything, but it's being punished along with the thief."

"It's only doing its duty as a good army donkey should," Pedro told him.

Suddenly he stopped laughing and looked about curiously. There was a change in the crowd's mood. The merriment was subsiding; attention was shifting from the spectacle in the field to a waterboy who had just come up with his laden burro. He was busily dispensing both water and information, the one for a price, the other free, and the suddenly serious faces of those nearest him indicated that he brought sobering news. Men were exchanging uncertain glances and crowding about the boy.

"What is it?" Pedro asked of no one in particular.

All around him the same question was being asked. The answer began filtering through the assemblage, passing from one man to another.

"Something's in the wind. They say there's going to be an attack on Granada. Word leaked out from headquarters."

"No, not an attack. Just a raid into the groves outside the city."

"It's the same thing. We'll meet as much resistance as if we tried to storm the walls."

The thief and the donkey were forgotten. Men began milling about, discussing the unexpected development. The crowd was thinning rapidly as groups moved off toward various parts of the camp, hoping to learn something more definite. Pedro turned to Felipe.

"I think I'll go back to The Nest. Marcos will probably know what the story is—he usually manages to get hold of inside information."

Felipe apparently didn't hear him. His eyes were narrowed as if in earnest thought, and he was plucking abstractedly at his beard. Pedro touched his arm.

"Felipe. . . ."

The man seemed to recollect himself. He nodded. "I'll get back to the hospital."

The two started back. Pedro was torn between uneasiness and excitement, now pondering what they had heard, now bursting into an impetuous flow of words. They walked together for a little way, then Pedro turned off toward The Nest with a pleasant parting remark. Felipe didn't answer, just smiled absently and waved his hand. The smile faded instantly and he looked grim and absorbed as he moved on.

It wasn't until then that Pedro suddenly realized that Felipe had scarcely spoken since they left the drillfield. Pedro hadn't even noticed, keyed up as he was. He sent a puzzled glance after his friend. Strange. Felipe seemed even more affected by the news than he was. Then excitement reclaimed Pedro and he hurried on toward the barracks.

As he moved along he sensed an air of agitation. Men were gathered in groups, and questions and speculations were flying back and forth. When he reached his unit's section he found the same excited discussions taking place. Marcos saw him coming and held up his hand to forestall his eager questions.

"All I know is what they're saying, Pedro. We're going to destroy that strip of parkland just outside Granada. At least, that's what the rumors say."

"The rumors are true enough," Andrés declared, his dour face showing an unwonted hint of animation. "I'm surprised we haven't raided that strip before now. A lot of that parkland is planted in gardens and orchards."

"Not enough to feed the city," someone pointed out.

"Enough for the city to fight for," Andrés retorted.

"Do you think there'll be a battle?" Paco asked, and one couldn't tell whether it was eagerness or anxiety that caused the breathless catch in his voice.

Marcos responded with a dry comment. "The Moors won't be sitting on their hands while we destroy their last source of food." His powerful voice was oddly subdued.

The rumors were confirmed officially the next morning. "The parklands that border Granada must be destroyed," the unit captain announced. "They not only contribute to the city's food supply, but the dense growths may screen enemy troop movements. The operation starts at dawn tomorrow. Meanwhile, be ready for further instructions." He hesitated, then added grimly, "And prepare for action."

There were no drills that day, nor even the usual camp tasks. Implements were issued for the demolition. Weapons were made ready. The troops stayed close to their quarters, visibly tense. They formed into groups, dispersed, formed other groups. There were sudden silences, sudden bursts of talk, now and then a flurry of laughter that didn't sound quite natural.

And men turned often toward the city, looking long and thoughtfully at the broad belt of greenery that bordered Granada's red walls.

The Parkland

Daybreak found the troops deployed in wide-ranged cordons, closing in toward the parkland. In full view of the enemy, they were tensed for action, expecting opposition at any moment. But no move came from the city, even when the vanguard of cavalry and infantry advanced into the shadows of the groves. This force was to station itself near the walls, to form a protective barrier between the workers and the city. The work crews followed at some distance. They carried axes and mattocks, but no weapons other than the knives which were part of their everyday equipment. Their job was to destroy the parkland; the armed advance guard would handle the fighting.

Pedro was with the work force. His heart was thumping as he approached the parkland. He told himself stoutly that he wasn't afraid, only properly alert to danger. But his heart kept right on thumping. He looked past the parkland to the walls rising beyond, so close that he could see turbaned heads at every battlement and tower.

"They're watching us," he said, his voice surprisingly steady, notwithstanding his tensed-up nerves.

"Of course." Chico was comfortingly matter-of-fact.

Paco sounded equally casual. "As long as they do no more than watch, we've nothing to worry about." But Pedro noticed that his jaw was tight-clamped, so that the muscles moved beneath the skin like shifting knots. Rodrigo too was taut-faced, his eyes narrowed to slits as he scanned the trees ahead.

All four had been assigned to the work force, which was made up largely of younger men, not so skilled with weapons but well fitted for strenuous labor. Battle-hardened veterans such as Marcos and Andrés were with the armed vanguard.

As they entered the parkland the view of the city was blocked by masses of vegetation. Even with danger lurking ahead, Pedro was conscious of the beauty of the place. On every hand stretched gardens and hedges, orchards and shady groves. Numerous towers, rising to tree-top level or higher, could be glimpsed through the intervening foliage. These, Pedro knew, were the pleasure lodges Felipe had told him of. The scene was peaceful and pleasant—until the orders were sounded.

"Level the place, men. Destroy everything—leave not even a bush standing."

They set to work. Soon the crash and crackle of falling trees mingled with their voices and the ring of their axes. There was still no sound from the city, but the workers remained tense, certain that the Moors would not let this bold move go unchallenged. Pedro found himself listening for an outburst of war cries, a sudden clangor of battle. It was heartening to know that a well-armed force protected the workers. Even so, those formidably manned walls were much too close for comfort.

Hard work dulled his uneasiness as the morning wore on. Pedro even found himself smiling with amusement when

Chico and Paco teamed up at their work, on the theory that joining forces would balance out their disparity in size. As Pedro finished demolishing a clump of hedge and moved on to another Rodrigo threw him a fleeting grin.

"What a way to fight a war!"

"How right you are!" Pedro called back. "I joined this army to fight Moors, not hedges."

But their flippancy was forced, and both knew it.

It was nearing noon, and the heat was mounting. Sweat beaded the men's faces and soaked their clothes, but they worked with scarcely a pause, driven by a sense of urgency. Felling trees, trampling gardens, uprooting vines and shrubs, they pushed their way through the green parkland and left a shambles behind. Tangles of foliage and broken branches covered the ground.

As the groves were leveled, the pleasure lodges which dotted the parkland stood out more openly. They were attractive structures, nearly all of similar design, surmounted by towers with balconies and latticed windows, set high to catch the air above the surrounding vegetation. Each lodge had its flower garden, and a small orchard. Hedge-bordered paths led from lodge to lodge.

The Moors—at least the wealthy ones—knew how to live graciously, Pedro thought.

At the edge of a treeless space he straightened and arched his tired back, shading his eyes against the sun. Far, far overhead a hawk sailed in lazy circles. It struck Pedro that the high-flying bird must see the world spread out like a vast map. What did it see in the city beyond the park? The thought drew his eyes toward the city, but it was invisible beyond the groves and hedges—invisible and silent. One wouldn't even know a city was there. Somehow its inaction seemed more ominous than a storm of defiance.

"It's strange they don't put up a fight," he observed to a nearby worker.

The other nodded. He was a pudgy fellow with squinty eyes and a pockmarked face. "I expected them to jump on us with everything they've got. Instead, they've done nothing but watch. It doesn't seem natural."

The man was plainly uneasy, and Pedro's earlier misgivings rose again as he moved on and attacked a grapevine, hung with clusters of small green grapes.

The workers were more widely scattered now. Some distance away Pedro saw Paco and Chico, still working as a team. Rodrigo was out of sight, somewhere among the masses of vegetation. Pedro found himself beside first one man, then another as he worked his way forward. A strange-looking army, he thought—barelegged, some shirtless, armed with axes and mattocks instead of weapons. He paused long enough to wolf down some bread and cheese, which each man had been provided with, then went on working.

Starting across an open stretch, he shouldered his ax, grateful for the brief respite. His path took him toward one of the lodges, and as he approached he looked at it with interest. The structure's picturesque charm accentuated the havoc around it, and suggested happier scenes. One could imagine children playing about the doorway, music and singing and laughter drifting from the high latticed windows in the tower. But now it was silent as death, deserted and—

Pedro caught his breath sharply. Deserted . . . ?

From the tower had come a brief bright flash. He halted and peered intently. Had he only imagined that fleeting gleam? Perhaps it was a sweat droplet shimmering on his eyelash, or a ray of sunlight reflected from the latticework. But it had looked more like the glint of metal. He shaded his eyes with his hand and scrutinized the tower. His heart contracted. Wasn't something moving behind that latticed window?

Suddenly a trumpet blared. An instant later, a tumultuous shout exploded.

"Allah-h akbar-r-r!"

The Moslem war cry came from everywhere at once, rising above the din of the devastation like the howl of a mighty storm. Latticed windows burst open and figures appeared, as if conjured by magic from the shadows within. Firearms barked, crossbows twanged; from every tower there was a deadly hail of balls and shafts.

For the first startled instant Pedro was unable to move. He heard the whiz and thud of missiles, saw men go limp and fall. Others broke into mad flight. He too started to run, then stopped short. Where could he go? The lodges were on all sides; to flee from one would only take him closer to another. He swept a frantic look about. Next to him lay a fallen tree. Flinging himself flat, he wormed himself under the leafy tangle of branches.

His thoughts raced, trying to grasp what had happened. Suddenly he understood. No wonder the city had been silent! The Moors had come out into the park before the Spaniards arrived, had lain hidden in the towers all morning, allowing the destruction to proceed until the workers were caught like

netted fish. The trapped men were unarmed, completely at
the mercy of the attackers. Expecting opposition from the
city, they had relied upon the advance guard for protection.
But the advance guard was engaged in a struggle near the
walls—its clash and clangor penetrated the tumult in the
immediate surroundings. Evidently an assault had been
launched from the city simultaneously with that from the
towers. Doubtless the powerful guard squadrons could repel
the assault—but what of the workers they were charged to
protect?

Warily Pedro peered through the leaves. The fallen tree
shielded him from the nearest lodge, but he was within sight
and range of others. The fact was suddenly emphasized as a
leaden ball thudded into the trunk, barely a foot from his
head. He looked about desperately. Some distance away a
half-demolished grove offered more substantial cover, but
missiles were flying thick in the intervening space. Even so,
workers were making for the trees, dodging from one clump
of bushes to another as they ran. Pedro measured the distance with his eyes, undecided whether to take the chance or
to stay where he was.

Footsteps pounded up and branches crackled as another
worker threw himself down beside him. Pedro recognized the
pockmarked man he'd been talking with a short while ago.
The pocked face was so pale it looked like pitted chalk. The
man lay panting for a moment, then pointed toward the
grove.

"Better make for those trees, lad. We'll have some chance
there—here we'll have none whatever."

Even as he spoke, a crossbow bolt ripped through the

foliage and imbedded its point in a branch. The man cringed visibly, but he screwed his face into a semblance of a grin. "I'll race you to the grove," he said.

Pedro felt no urge to joke, but he too managed a twisted grin. "I'm with you," he said, tensing his muscles for the dash.

They ran like mad for the nearest clump of vegetation, crouched there briefly, then sped on toward the next, spurred by the menacing hum and thud of missiles. Pedro's eyes were fixed on the grove that promised them sanctuary. It was just ahead now, looming up to his sweat-blurred vision as a vague green shimmer. They were nearly there when a searing pain stabbed through his leg. With a sharp cry, he lunged forward and fell.

Pedro clutched at his leg convulsively. His hand felt the warm wetness of blood. It was streaming from the side of his leg, just above the knee. He gave the wound a quick, stunned look, then clenched his teeth against the pain and started dragging himself on toward the grove. His companion had already reached their goal. Now, crouched by a cluster of shrubbery, he glanced back and saw Pedro. His pitted face sagged. For the briefest of instants he seemed to hesitate, then he abandoned his shelter and dashed back. Stooping, he grasped Pedro's arm to help him upright.

"Just a little farther, lad. We're nearly th—"

The man's grasp went suddenly slack, and a hoarse gasp broke from his throat. He crumpled forward, his body striking Pedro's, then rolled over onto the grass. Pedro gave a cry of horror. The man lay in an awkward heap, his face upturned, blood coming from a wound in his head. The eyes were open, but Pedro knew that they couldn't see and would never see again.

Pedro stared at the still form, dazed by shock and pain. For a moment he remained motionless. Then with an effort he gathered his faculties. The man was beyond help. He must get to cover. Doggedly he started on toward the grove.

Suddenly he became aware that missiles were no longer striking near him, though the firing hadn't stopped. With a leap of hope he saw that the soldiers of the guard force were swarming into the area. The Moors in the towers had shifted their fire from the weaponless workers and turned its full power on the armed men in an attempt to drive them back. Workers, taking advantage of the respite, were hurrying from all sides to the shelter of the grove, some supporting wounded comrades. One of them bent over the pockmarked man, peered into the bloodied face, then shook his head and stooped to lift Pedro.

"Come along, *compañero*. You'll be safer in the grove."

The man helped Pedro toward the trees amid a melee of shouting and running. The guard troops were stationing themselves around the towers, in whatever shelter they could find among the demolished trees and hedges, their crossbows and firearms answering the volleys from the barricaded Moors. In the grove, men were giving what care they could to the wounded, for none could be taken to the rear through that withering fire.

Pedro's helper eased him to the ground among several other wounded men and examined the bleeding furrow scored in his leg. "Crossbow bolt," he muttered. "You're lucky at that, lad. It's a long gash, but not very deep. A bit farther inward and it would've shattered the bone." Pedro shuddered at the thought. "We'll need a bandage," the man said, then added, "This will do," and proceeded to rip the sleeve from Pedro's shirt. The sweat-soaked cloth was scarcely an ideal bandage, but it would help check the bleeding, and this was no time to be fussy.

Pedro sat with the leg outstretched stiffly and tried to ignore the pain. He looked back toward where the pockmarked man's body lay, partly visible through the trees. Just a few minutes ago that soldier had been talking with him. Now he was dead. Pedro still couldn't grasp the thought. That pockmarked face was faintly familiar, but he didn't know the man, and was sure the man hadn't known him. Yet he had braved a hail of deadly missiles to give him aid—and died in consequence. Pedro whispered a prayer for the soldier's soul—a noble and courageous soul, surely, however ill-favored his pudgy body and pitted face.

From everywhere came the sounds of battle, some close and ear-splitting, some dulled by distance. For this was no single conflict—rather, a separate combat was raging in every grove and garden throughout the parkland.

"*Allah-h akbar-r-r!*" The Moslem war cry sounded repeatedly through the clang and clatter.

"*Santia-a-a-go!*" The answering cry of the Spaniards mingled with the Moors' fierce shouts.

From time to time soldiers stumbled into the grove, helping wounded comrades to some measure of safety. A riderless horse came charging through the brush, its flanks red with the blood of its fallen rider. The trees and bushes afforded partial cover, but stray missiles tore through the growth with

ominous frequency. The unarmed workers could do nothing
to aid in the fighting. They could only crouch and watch.
Pedro noticed with incredulous surprise that he still had his
ax, his hand clamped upon it like a vise. It took an effort to
loosen his grasp and lay the implement aside.

A triumphant shout came from one of the workers. "Look
—we're smoking the devils out!"

Spanish crossbows were loosing bolts tipped with burning
pitch against the towers. The bolts streaked through the air
like fire-streaming comets, and their effect was devastating.
Already the nearest lodge was afire, and turbaned warriors
were frantically spilling from the doorway. As Pedro watched,
a tongue of flame leaped up from another tower, and presently the fiery columns could be seen rising in scores of
places.

As the Moors were driven from the lodges, the nature of
the combat altered. The exchange of volleys from cover gave
way to open battle, the adversaries meeting and mingling,
hand-to-hand, sword against scimitar. Around the grove the
melee surged and shifted as the contenders pressed forward
or fell back. Once the struggle broke through the fringes of
the grove; fighting units merged with work crews, and axes
were put to use as weapons. Pedro pulled himself upright,
propped against a tree, his ax held ready. But the conflict
receded without reaching the group of wounded men.

Gradually the shifting turmoil began to move steadily
toward the city. The Moors were being relentlessly driven
back. Their resistance ended with startling suddenness.
There came a fleeting silence, like a momentary lull in a
storm; then as if at a signal the Moslems broke and fled. In

pell-mell confusion the remnants of their army rushed past the grove, yelling Spaniards close at their heels.

A wounded man beside Pedro raised himself on an elbow. "Scurry for your holes, like the rats you are!" he shouted, then lay back down with a low moan.

Pedro felt himself trembling, whether from weakness or pain or sheer relief he didn't know. He reached for his water flask and gulped down a long draught. The sounds of flight and pursuit were receding rapidly toward the city, but bursts of firing from other points showed that fighting still raged in scattered spots. The crouching workers straightened and looked at one another uncertainly. One of them indicated the injured men.

"We've got to get these men to the hospital, and the sooner the better."

Some of the men hurried to give assistance to the wounded; others gripped their axes and turned back to the interrupted work. Pedro, his mind swimming, felt a sustaining hand grasp his arm. "Can you walk if I help you?" a voice asked.

"I can hobble," Pedro said grimly.

The devastation was already being resumed, and even as Pedro stumbled away, leaning awkwardly upon his helper, the sound of axes began mingling with the distant gunfire. The din of conflict seemed concentrated just outside the city's walls, as if the fleeing Moors had rallied for a last desperate stand there. Pedro looked back worriedly.

"The battle isn't over yet," he said, his voice thick with pain and exhaustion.

"It is for you," his helper said dryly.

Again—the Queen's Hospital

Pedro awoke gradually. Even when he was fully awake he kept his eyes closed for a while, reluctant to face reality. Sleep had been fitful, but it had brought periods of merciful escape from pain. He wanted to cling to it, and blot out the memory of the previous day.

Stretcher-men had started rescuing the wounded even while the battle still raged, but Pedro, supported by his companion, had hobbled nearly to the camp before a stretcher was available, for many men were in far worse condition than he. Scores of wounded were already at the hospital when he was brought in; others had still been arriving. After his wound was attended to he had alternately slept in exhaustion and lain wakeful with pain. But the pain wasn't so bad now. The sharp throbbing had subsided to an ache that was constant but bearable.

Presently he opened his eyes. Canvas sloped overhead, and rows of cots stretched on either side, nearly all of them occupied. This wasn't the main hospital tent, made familiar by his visits with Felipe, but one of the five adjoining tents, unused until now. Men with less serious injuries had been brought here, while the critically wounded were taken to the main tent.

Pedro raised himself on an elbow and looked about, filled with commiseration at the sight of the bandaged heads and limbs and bodies. If the men's hurts weren't critical, they were far from trivial. In the farthest corner he recognized a man from his unit, but saw no other familiar face. As he lay back, he fetched a dismal sigh, whereupon a cheerful voice spoke from the adjoining cot.

"Come now, lad. Heh! Things *can't* be as bad as all that."

The speaker was sitting on the edge of the cot, a spare little man with one arm in a sling, clad only in a pair of ragged breeches. His skinny body seemed to be all bumps and knobs—knobby shoulders, knobby elbows, knobby knees and ankles. His face followed the same pattern—chin and cheekbones were rounded knobs that protruded too far, while his nose was a rounded knob that didn't protrude far enough. Even his shiny-bald skull was knoblike.

His lips quirked into a smile as he caught Pedro's eye. "Don't look so glum, lad. You'll be up and out of here before you know it."

Pedro forced an answering smile. "Oh, that isn't what I'm worrying about. It's just that. . . ." He trailed the words off and finished with a shrug.

"I know. It's just that you're wounded and miserable and far from home. But being wounded isn't so bad. Heh! No work. No responsibilities. Nothing to do but sleep, like my barrel-bellied friend there." He eyes moved on past Pedro, and he gestured with his unbandaged arm.

Pedro, following the gesture, turned toward the cot on his other side. It was occupied by a chubby man with bandages swathing all one side of his face and part of the other, leaving only an eye, a nose, and a small patch of cheek visible. The eye had been closed, but now it flickered open and a muffled voice came from behind the bandages.

"You can call ne darrel-dellied, but don't clain ne as a sriend—it endarrasses ne." Obviously he couldn't move his lips, which made certain consonants impossible to enunciate.

The knobby man winked at Pedro. "Just listen to him! A crossbow bolt shaved his jaw closer than any barber's razor ever could. Now he talks like a man with a mouthful of mush."

The stout man fixed his visible eye on the other's bandaged arm. "You detter look out, or I'll stot talking and wrat zhose dandages around your zhroat."

Pedro understood. The rough banter was a sham, a show of courage to keep from losing courage. Making light of each other's hurts helped make them bearable. He took his cue accordingly.

"Vaya!" He chuckled. "It's lucky they put me between you two. Maybe I can keep you apart."

His light manner was forced, but it made him feel better, so much so that he decided to sit upright. That was a mistake, for at once his leg started throbbing again. Pedro drew the sheet aside and saw that the wound was neatly bandaged, and gave off a faint odor of wine and oil. Strange, he could scarcely remember its being treated; he must have been near fainting at the time. He felt shaky now that he was sitting up, and the surroundings had a tendency to wobble, so he lay down again.

The stout man's uncovered eye was turned toward him.

"What gaze you zhat wound—an arquedus dall or a crossdow dolt?"

"I'm not sure which—I didn't think to examine it as it went past. But whatever it was, it gave me a neat nick."

"De zhanksul it was no nore zhan a—"

"Hey! Breakfast! About time!" The interruption came from the knobby man. An orderly had appeared with a huge and well-laden tray. He placed it on the surgical chest and went back for more, while the abler patients began serving their bedfast comrades. The knobby man jumped up.

"I'll get yours for you, lad—you'd better stay off that leg. And you too, Barrel-belly. Heh! It'd be all gone before you could waddle across the tent."

The little man scuttled back and forth a few times and supplied them with bread and steaming gruel, at the sight of which Pedro realized suddenly that his stomach was a gnawing hollow. He downed the food gratefully, feeling almost guilty at his own enjoyment as he watched the stout man trying to eat. The poor fellow had a problem, being obliged to insert morsels past the edge of the bandage into the corner of his mouth.

"Heh!" His friend snickered. "Reminds me of someone trying to fill a bag with the drawstring closed tight." But the sympathy in his bumpy face belied the derisive words.

Pedro looked up eagerly whenever anyone came into the tent, hoping to see Felipe. That wasn't likely, of course. Felipe would be in the main tent as always, lending a hand to the work there, unaware that Pedro was in the hospital. He wished he could be sure his barrackmates were all right. There was no way to find out, with everything in such a bustle. Maybe when the confusion settled a bit he could hobble into the other tent and see for himself.

With his breakfast tucked away, Pedro felt considerably stronger, and was relieved to find that the surroundings wobbled only slightly when he sat up. He was surprised that the general mood seemed not at all melancholy. He heard low moans now and then, but there was a constant hum of cheerful conversation. His neighbor with the injured arm offered a comment.

"Quite a tentful—heh, lad? But there are more men nursing wounds in Granada than there are here, you can count on that." He uncrossed his knobby knees and recrossed them in reverse position. "I'll give the Moslem devils credit for one thing, though—they really put up a fight. And none more than Boabdil himself."

"Boabdil took part in the battle?"

The knoblike head bobbed up and down. "He commanded the Moorish cavalry personally, and was the last to retreat when we drove them back into the city. Heh! I've heard him called some uncomplimentary names, but no one can call him a coward."

The stout man's muffled voice corroborated the statement. "Doaddil was in zhe zhick oz zhe dattle sron start to sinish."

"Even after they holed up in the city they kept up a barrage from the walls, but we could stay out of range of that." The little man glanced at his sling and shook his head ruefully. "Only trouble was, I didn't get out of range quite fast enough."

"Did we finish leveling the parkland?" Pedro asked.

"That we did, right up to the edge of their range of fire. Outside of that, there isn't a sprig left standing." He looked at Pedro questioningly. "I take it you were in the work crew—heh, lad?"

"Yes, but I was put out of action just after the fighting started. I got too close to one of those pleasure lodges."

An angry snort sounded behind the stout man's bandages. "Tleasure lodges—and zhey were hiding an arny! Trust zhose sneaky Noors to tull a trick like zhat."

The knobby man's voice took on a sudden hard edge. "They knew we were coming before we even started. They must have been hiding since long before dawn. And we walked right into the trap!"

The words struck Pedro forcibly. It was true—Boabdil's troops had been lying in wait for hours, some in the pleasure lodges, some behind the city's walls. The trap had been laid with cunning and sprung with precision. Obviously it had been carefully planned before the ravages started.

Pedro lay back on his cot, bewildered by the thought. It hadn't even occurred to him before. He'd been too overwhelmed by shock and misery. He saw it plainly now—the Moors certainly had known the Spaniards' intentions, and well beforehand. But how had they learned?

He turned a puzzled face to his neighbor. "How do you suppose they found out what we were planning?"

"Who knows? 'The wind has a tongue,' so the saying goes." He looked grim for a moment, then his knobby shoulders lifted in a shrug. "However they learned, they didn't stop us."

There was an interval of silence. Suddenly the man looked
past Pedro and he jerked his head toward the tent entrance.
"Heh! Time to get our scratches oiled."

A small group of barber-surgeons had come in, their red-
rimmed eyes evidencing sleepless hours at their tasks. Not all
were of the hospital staff, for in this emergency, company
barbers had also been pressed into service. Weary-looking
apprentices accompanied them, carrying trays of instruments,
bandages, and evil-smelling lotions.

Pedro, when it came his turn, got fresh bandages on his leg
and a brusque assurance that his stay in the hospital would
be brief. "Just a scratch," was the surgeon's appraisal of the
wound. "Lucky you were barelegged. When a shaft goes
through clothing, it's apt to push threads and bits of cloth
into a wound. Causes trouble sometimes. Nothing like that
here—you'll be limping for a while, but you'll be fit for light
duty in a few days."

It was welcome news to Pedro. He settled back on the cot,
his leg smarting afresh after the treatment. Again he wondered uneasily if any of his barrackmates had been injured.
He toyed with the thought of hobbling over to the other
tents to check, but realized at once that it wouldn't be
permitted—the hospital couldn't have patients wandering
from tent to tent. Anyway, he'd doubtless see some of his
comrades later in the day, if visitors were allowed. Brighten-
ing at the possibility, he ventured to question a passing
orderly. The response was explosive.

"*Visitors?*" The orderly was harried, and in no amiable
mood. "There'll be no visitors today. As if we haven't enough

to contend with, without cluttering up the tent with visitors!" Then, seeing Pedro's disappointment, he relented somewhat. "Tomorrow, probably, when things settle down a bit."

Tomorrow seemed a week away, Pedro thought morosely.

The day wore on. The men talked, and cracked rough jokes, and tried to suppress moans. Pedro conversed sporadically with his two neighbors, and listened with amusement as they exchanged their genial insults. The knobby man was there only at intervals; more often he was scurrying about the tent, making himself useful at small tasks or talking to patients. He was a restless fellow. His stout friend was understandably less talkative, and though his injury didn't keep him on his cot, he showed no inclination to leave it. For long periods he would lie motionless, apparently asleep.

The July sun beat down on the overhead canvas, and the heat grew oppressive. An orderly circled the tent and raised the sides to let in some stir of air, in case any air should be stirring. Pedro, trying to ignore the heat and the smart of his wound, fixed his attention on the murmur of conversation around him. The talk was mainly concerned with yesterday's battle, especially the Moors' well-laid trap.

"Beyond doubt they'd been warned," someone said. "How else could they have known?"

"Of course. Some scoundrel betrayed our plan beforehand. I'd gladly take another wound to find out who it was."

"A Moslem spy, most likely. Or maybe even one of our own men, turned traitor for the sake of a reward."

The last possibility shocked Pedro. Yet, he knew, such

things had happened before. Somberly he looked about at
the rows of sufferers. However the Moors had obtained their
information, they had used it with frightful results.

Absorbed in his thoughts, Pedro almost failed to notice an
orderly who had come into the tent with a stack of cloth for
bandages. He was placing the linen swathes in the surgical
chest when Pedro recognized him as Felipe's attendant. The
orderly turned at Pedro's call, and his fatigue-drawn face
brightened into a smile that was half cheerful, half concerned.

"What's this, *amigo?* Did you stop one of those Moslem
bolts too?"

Pedro returned the smile. "I didn't exactly stop it, but
maybe I slowed it a bit as it went by."

"*Caray!* You must be fond of this hospital. You can't
seem to keep away from the place."

"That's right. I like it so much I decided to move in."
Pedro eagerly hitched himself to a sitting position. "Look,
may I ask a favor? When you get back to the main tent, will
you tell Felipe Luza that I'm here—and very anxious to see
him?"

The orderly looked at him strangely. "I'd be glad to tell
him. Only he isn't there."

"Isn't there? Why, where is he?"

"That's what I've been wanting to ask *you*. He was with
you, the last time I saw him."

Pedro stared, uncomprehending. The orderly went on.
"You two left the hospital together—remember? You said
you were going for a stroll. Three days ago, that was. I
haven't seen him since."

Pedro's jaw dropped. He shook his head slowly, incredulously. "But—but we only spent an hour or so together. Then he started back to the hospital."

"Maybe he started, but he never got here." The orderly turned up his palms in a baffled gesture. "He's gone, that's all—don't ask me where or why. I thought maybe you knew something, but I can see you don't. There probably would've been a fuss raised, but with so much happening all at once. . . ." He shrugged expressively and fell silent for a moment. Then he turned away. "I've got to get back—we're up to our ears in work, you know."

Pedro stared after him, numb with bewilderment. He passed his hand slowly across his face, as if dragging away a cobweb. It just didn't make sense. Felipe gone? Just like that? It *couldn't* be.

He thought back to that afternoon—was it only three days ago?—when he'd last seen Felipe. At that time Felipe surely had no intention of leaving. He'd been his usual cheerful self, at least until. . . . Carefully, minutely, Pedro reviewed the occasion. The pleasant stroll. Their laughing over the thief and the donkey. Then the news of the invasion of the parkland, and Felipe's sudden grim absorption. His change of mood had been swift and surprising, but surely it had nothing to do with. . . .

Snatches of the talk around him intruded vaguely into Pedro's consciousness. ". . . someone betrayed us . . . they'd planted a spy in our camp . . . doubtless here all along . . . gathering information. . . ."

An agonizing thought began to rise. Pedro pushed it from his mind before it could even take shape. But it rose again, not to be denied, and a cold hand seemed to close over his heart.

Pedro lay back and covered his face with his arms. Many things had suddenly become clear.

Tragic News

Pedro lay long awake that night, and not just from the pain of his wound. His heart ached with bitterness and disillusionment. Over and over he relived his friendship with Felipe; over and over he sought for some hope, some saving doubt. Perhaps it wasn't Felipe who had warned the Moors. Perhaps there was some other explanation for his disappearance. Perhaps. . . .

It was no use. It was time to face facts, he told himself miserably. He had half suspected from the start that Felipe wasn't what he claimed. Many things had pointed to the truth, small things in themselves, but linked together they made a heavy chain of evidence—Felipe's frequent lapses into Arabic, his tolerant attitude toward the Moors, his obvious unfamiliarity with European clothing. Why, he had scarcely bothered to hide his admiration for the Moor, Tarfe.

Pedro recalled Felipe's evasiveness about his personal history. It was only after he'd had time to concoct a plausible story that he'd given any information whatever. Claiming Zahara as his home had been clever—no one could prove that statement false, for Zahara's inhabitants had been either slain or taken captive ten years before. That was a conveniently lengthy period for Felipe—long enough to make his assumed identity impossible to trace and verify.

Looking back, Felipe's story seemed glaringly transparent. Why hadn't he seen through it at once? Yet, others also had been deceived—even don Gonzalo de Córdova. But then, don Gonzalo hadn't become Felipe's close companion. Pedro felt a vague sense of guilt. Time and again he'd had doubts and suspicions. Should he have taken them to someone higher up? Had he done so, would that battle in the park have been averted?

Sleep came at last, but it was troubled and fitful.

He felt better in the morning. Amid the sound and stir in the tent he could close his mind to the distressing thoughts. But whenever the talk turned to the battle—and it did so often—bitterness would again well up in him. It must have showed in his face, for the knobby man began looking at him keenly, and presently made an obvious attempt to rouse his spirits.

"Heh, lad," he said suddenly, "if our mush-mouthed friend there will sing us a song, will you favor us with a dance?"

Pedro summoned a quick grin and a light response, feeling ashamed for showing his gloomy feelings. Stop moping, he told himself. You're not the only one with troubles—just look around you. So you've lost a friend! All right, you've still got plenty of others. Resolutely, he faced the new day with a show of cheerfulness.

There was less harried activity in the tent today. The wounded, having been treated and made as comfortable as possible, now needed only routine care, while time and nature healed and strengthened. After the surgeons had made their mid-morning rounds, Pedro started hobbling about a bit. Each awkward step cost him a twinge of pain, but he kept it up at intervals, hoping that a show of activity would speed his release to duty. Men talked, or dozed, or moved about restlessly, or lay in quiet resignation.

It was going to be a sweltering day. Already the heat was mounting, and it wasn't yet noon. The side walls were still raised, but not a breath of air came through. Pedro thought longingly of The Nest, with its fretwork of branches that let in the air and its brushy thatching that held out the sun. For summer comfort, canvas couldn't compare with brushwood.

With the noon meal came an announcement that visitors would be admitted later in the afternoon. The patients' eager response made Pedro realize that others besides himself were waiting anxiously for word from comrades. Those comrades might be safe in the camp, or they might be lying wounded in another tent. They may have been among the slain. There was no way to know.

Pedro was restless with impatience and anxiety. He sat up, lay back down, sat up again, got out of the cot, got back in, all the while keeping an expectant eye on the tent entrance. His knobby neighbor watched him with an amused smile.

"Simmer down, lad, simmer down. Heh! It'll be a good two hours before they let any visitors in."

Before Pedro could reply, a shout sounded just outside the entrance, and an orderly burst into the tent as if he'd been kicked in from behind. His voice was shrill with excitement.

"It's the Queen! Her Highness herself!"

Those in the tent looked at him blankly, not grasping his meaning. The orderly fairly screeched.

"It's the Queen, I say! Doña Isabella! Coming to visit the hospital—she's on the way right now."

The other attendants gasped. "*Caramba*—and just look at this tent!" "Sweep out that litter—quick!" "Get that soiled laundry out of sight!"

The man who had brought the warning yelled an order to the patients who were up and about. "Back to your cots!" He flapped his hands wildly, like a housewife shooing out chickens which have invaded her kitchen. "It's the Queen, I tell you—you can't meet the Queen without anything on!"

The patients hastily returned to their cots, slid under the sheets, and drew them decorously up to their chins. Attendants rushed about, putting things to order. Surgeons hurried in to make an anxious check, then hurried out to be ready to greet the royal visitor. In a few minutes, as if a wizard had waved his wand, the tent presented an edifying appearance of neatness—provided one didn't look too close. One of the orderlies had a last-minute admonition for the patients.

"Listen, everybody! If the Queen should speak to you— and she probably will—remember to address her as 'Your Highness.' You can pretend to be well-bred, even if you aren't."

Someone dashed outside to investigate, then dashed back in again. "Her Highness is in the main tent now. She'll be here most any minute." He stationed himself at the tent entrance and stood peeking out, ready to give a warning signal.

A long wait followed. Eyes were glued to the tent entrance. Ears were strained for approaching footsteps. There were nervous coughs, low whispers, a snicker or two. At last the lookout whirled about, so suddenly that he nearly lost his balance.

"She's coming!"

His intended whisper was so loud with excitement that it must have reached the royal ears. The attendants bowed low. Pedro's heart thumped like a drum as he looked over the bent backs and watched the Queen enter. She made a regal picture, though she was dressed simply in a dark-green gown, with a plain coif drawn over her coppery-gold hair. Only a handful of pages formed her escort.

Doña Isabella moved along the rows of cots, offering a word of sympathy here, an encouraging smile there, spending a few minutes with each man in turn. With Pedro, doubtless because of his youth, the Queen was especially gracious. When she asked his name, Pedro was so flustered that he tripped over his answer.

"P-Pedro, Your Highness. Pedro Tegero."

"I hope your injury is not serious, Pedro."

"Oh, no, Your Highness. Not at all." The concern in her face was so patently sincere that he felt he should add further assurance. "Why, really, Your Highness, I've been hurt worse than this when I fell off the wall at La Rábida."

The Queen looked amused, but her eyes lighted with interest. "La Rábida? You are familiar with La Rábida?"

"I lived there, Your Highness. All my life, until this spring when I joined your army."

"Ah! Then you know Fray Juan Pérez, of course?"

Pedro's eyes widened in surprise. So the Queen knew Fray Juan! He answered eagerly. "Oh, yes, Your Highness. I know him well—very well. He has been a wonderful friend to me."

Doña Isabella smiled. "It seems we have a mutual friend, Pedro. I have known and respected Fray Juan for years. In fact, he was once my spiritual advisor."

"Your Highness! I didn't know that!" Pedro blurted, then colored as he realized how brash the words sounded. But the Queen smiled again, and as she moved on added a parting remark.

"When you see Fray Juan again, Pedro, tell him he is often in my thoughts."

Pedro looked after her through a rosy glow. Wonder of wonders! He, Pedro Tegero, insignificant nobody, had actually conversed with Isabella of Castile, Queen of Spain! And, even more amazing, they had a mutual friend, dear to them both!

Pedro had known the prior of La Rábida for as long as he could remember, yet never had he heard Fray Juan mention that he was acquainted with the Queen. Any worldly man would have made much of the fact. To the humble Franciscan, a sovereign and a servant were equally important, both being children of God, and he a "little brother" to each.

An excited babble burst out following the Queen's departure, each man proudly recounting his brief personal exchange with doña Isabella. Throbbing wounds were ignored for the moment. After all, it isn't every day that a lowly soldier talks with a queen. One of the men found himself the butt of some playful banter. Overcome with awe in the royal presence, he had fumbled his etiquette and addressed the Queen simply as "Señora," rather than "Your Highness." He looked sheepish for a while, but soon perked up.

"Doña Isabella didn't seem to mind. There's no reason I should."

"I've heard," someone observed, "that in some country or other—France, I think it is—the queen is addressed as 'Your Majesty.' The king too, of course."

"Hm-m. That sounds a bit grander than 'Your Highness.'"

"Yes. And a great deal grander than 'Señora.'"

The excitement soon subsided, for the men were still waiting anxiously for news of friends, and even a queen takes second place to a friend. A buzz of voices could be heard from outside the hospital compound. There too, men were waiting anxiously, seeking admittance to look for injured comrades. Presently an orderly announced that the visitors could come in. "Only a few at a time," he stipulated. "If we let everybody in at once, we'd have to move the patients out to make room."

Pedro sat up on the edge of his cot, careful of his injured leg, hopefully noting each visitor who entered. Almost at once the knobby man spied an acquaintance and dashed away from his cot to greet him. Then the stout man's muffled voice called to a visitor, who understandably failed to recognize him until he identified himself, whereupon they started chatting. Pedro had to wait considerably longer, but at last a familiar lanky form passed through the entrance.

"Over here, Paco," Pedro called eagerly.

"Pedro! So there you are!" Paco hurried over. His face filled with concern as he looked at the bandaged leg. "Is it bad, fellow?" he asked.

"It's nothing—just a scratch." Pedro swiftly scanned his friend's face. Something he saw there sent a sudden premonition clutching at his heart. "Are you all right? And the others?"

Paco let the questions pass. "Thank God you're not hurt worse. We've been worried." He looked back toward the tent entrance. "Chico will be here in a few minutes. He's in the next tent, looking for you. We separated to save time— they'll only let us stay a few minutes."

Pedro felt partially relieved. "So you two are all right. What about the others?"

Again Paco looked toward the entrance, as if he wanted to avoid the question. But his manner was itself an answer, and Pedro grasped his arm anxiously. "The others, Paco?"

Paco faced him then, but still was silent for a moment. At last he spoke, his voice low and husky.

"Marcos is dead, Pedro."

Pedro's body went slack with shock. He stared at his friend almost in unbelief. Paco went on, his tone curiously dull and expressionless.

"It happened when the Moors made their first assault from the walls. Andrés saw him fall. They were fighting side by side."

For a moment the two looked at each other in silence. Then Pedro's eyes misted and he turned away.

"God rest his soul," he murmured in a choked voice.

Paco drew a long breath. "It's hard to believe. You know a man for weeks, live with him, learn to like him—and then. . . ." His words trailed off into another brief silence. Abruptly his manner changed, becoming firm and self-possessed. "These things have to be faced. Marcos was a soldier. He died a soldier's death."

Pedro swallowed hard. Then with an effort he got hold of himself. Paco was right. These things had to be faced. "Were there others from our unit killed?" he asked.

"Some. I don't know how many. No one that I knew well, but Rodrigo lost a close friend." Paco shook his head soberly. "It seems a miracle there weren't even more casualties, the way we were caught unprepared. Chico and I were lucky—we were in the middle of a thick grove when the battle started." He looked again toward the entrance. "Here comes Chico now."

Chico's normally placid manner showed mingled concern and relief as he greeted Pedro. The three had only a few minutes together before the tent was cleared of visitors, so that others waiting outside could be admitted. "We'll be back tomorrow, if they'll let us," Chico promised as he turned away, then added, "Andrés and Rodrigo too." Paco explained, "A few a day from each unit—that's all they'll allow."

When they had gone, Pedro sat unmoving, sick with misery. Marcos dead? It didn't seem possible. Marcos had become so familiar, so much a part of life here in camp. If only he could be alone for a while—he needed solitude to cope with this blow. But the tent was continually astir with men filing through in search of comrades. Acquaintances from his unit appeared from time to time and exchanged a few words with him in passing. Each made some regretful reference to Marcos. The big man had been well known and well liked in the unit.

Pedro had himself in hand by the time the last of the visitors left. The men in the adjoining cots were exchanging their customary insults, but he detected a subdued note in their banter, and wondered if they too had heard saddening news. If so, they made no mention of it, and Pedro determined to maintain a similar reticence. Whatever one's feelings might be, this wasn't the time nor the place to air them.

Sunset struck a ruddy glow through the sloping canvas overhead. The day's heat still hung on, but a breeze had sprung up and promised relief. The evening meal was brought in, and appreciative comments greeted the well-laden platters. Hospital fare was always better than normal army rations—the Queen saw to that—but tonight there was a special treat of fruit and other delicacies.

"Her Highness never visits the hospital empty-handed," one of the orderlies explained.

"I'll wager that the staff got its share first," someone said, half joking, half accusing.

"That's an unwarranted insult," the orderly said with a fine show of indignation. Then he added with a sly grin, "Be sure to try the spiced cakes—they're delicious."

The food meant little to Pedro in his present mood, but he ate dutifully. In silent sympathy he watched the stout man trying to feed himself. The poor fellow struggled valiantly for a while, then gave up and pushed the food aside.

"Just ny luck!" he said plaintively, seeming undecided whether to sigh or chuckle. "A sutter sit sor zhe king hinselz, and I can't ezen eat it."

"You can afford to miss a meal, Barrel-belly," the knobby man bantered. But Pedro knew that the banter was really camouflaged sympathy.

The meal over, Pedro sat on the edge of his cot and conversed with his two oddly-matched neighbors. Now and then he flexed his injured leg tentatively. It was less painful now, or else he'd become so inured to the pain that it was less noticeable. Darkness had gathered, and the lamps were lighted. The breeze had strengthened and become quite brisk, sweeping under the upraised tent walls in refreshing whiffs.

"What a breeze!" the knobby man exclaimed. "And what a meal! The way I feel right now, if I were a cat I'd be purring."

"Is I were a cat, I'd de looking sor a nouse. I'n still hungry," the pudgy man complained.

It hadn't been a normal day, and tonight the normal routine was relaxed, the talk continuing well past the usual hour. But presently, when even the muffled sounds from the camp outside had subsided, the lamps were dimmed and the murmur of talk died into silence.

Pedro lay wakeful. The thought of Marcos, suppressed until now, came back with fresh intensity. Poignant memories drifted through his mind, some that made his throat tighten, some that brought a faint sad smile to his lips. He had known Marcos less than three months, but he would remember him for a lifetime.

Pedro's shock at the news was gone now; he could face the fact and accept it. Marcos was dead. God rest his soul.

How much had happened since the troops marched out to the parkland, less than three days ago! He recalled the leveling of the groves, the fear and fury of the battle, the agonizing journey back to camp, the hours which had ensued. He had lost two dear friends, Marcos and Felipe. He remembered with a curious indifference that he had conversed with the Queen of Spain. In this moment it seemed a petty thing.

Pedro drew a long slow breath. It had been a harrowing period, with one tragic blow crowded close upon another. But it was over now, he consoled himself. The train of calamities had run its course; now would come the calm that follows the storm. On that comforting thought he drifted into sleep.

It was a restless sleep—and a short one.

A commotion outside abruptly shattered the stillness. Pedro's eyes snapped open; he sat bolt upright in startled alarm. A stir moved through the dimly lit tent; men spoke in puzzled, half-awake voices. They heard shouts outside, the sounds of running feet, an ominous crackling noise. Then suddenly, from everywhere at once, a frantic cry burst out.

"Fire!"

Disaster

"All right, clear the tent, everybody! Get out before you're burned out." The orderly's manner was determinedly casual, but there was a telltale quaver in his voice. With valiant cheerfulness he added, "Better wrap a sheet around you as you go—you might meet some ladies out there."

His air of nonchalance fooled nobody, but it did have a steadying effect. Hastily but without panic the men slid out of the cots. Some crawling, some hobbling, some leaning on abler comrades, they groped their way out of the dimly lighted tent. Pedro, snatching the sheet from his cot, dragged it after him as he crawled under the updrawn canvas wall, heedless of the pain of his wound. As he did so, he heard a desperate shout from the adjoining tent.

"Get the bedridden men out—and in God's name, *fast!*"

Never in life would he forget the scene which met his eyes as he came into the open. The court precinct was a mass of flames. They slashed the black sky with lurid orange, threw a pulsing glare over the surroundings, filled the night with a crackling roar.

"*Dios mio!*" The words burst from his lips in an involuntary cry.

Everywhere was confusion and tumult. People were stum-

bling frantically out of the court precinct, some hastily pull-
ing on clothing, some not even noticing their lack of it.
Screaming women ran to and fro aimlessly or clung to one
another in terror. A few men had grabbed up weapons but
stood bewildered, not knowing on whom they could turn
them. Picketed horses reared and plunged, mad with fear.

The fire, fanned by the wind, was spreading with terrifying
speed. Already it had swept from the court precinct into the
surrounding areas, the flames leaping from tent to tent. Their
heat struck Pedro's skin with searing force.

An instinctive thought leaped into his mind. "The Moors!"
he exclaimed aloud.

"*The Moors!*" The words could be heard on all sides.
Everyone had the same thought: this was a trick of the
enemy—somehow the Moors had contrived to start the fire.

Orderlies and surgeons were carrying the helpless wounded
from the main hospital tent. Pedro limped toward them,
wanting to help, but was roughly thrust back.

"One side, fellow—you're only in the way."

He realized at once that it was true; in his crippled condition he would only hinder the efforts. He hobbled away,
exasperated at his uselessness, still dragging his sheet along.
Suddenly noticing it, he drew it about him and moved
painfully toward the street which skirted the hospital compound. If he couldn't work, at least he could be watchful.
The Moors might attack at any minute.

From the edge of the street he could see to the camp's
borders. There was teeming activity everywhere as men
strove desperately to stem the spread of the fire. Some were

forming bucket lines from the river bank. Others were dashing water against the tents from the huge casks in the camp. Grooms and mule-drivers were trying to get fear-maddened animals to safety. Off in the artillery ground, scores of soldiers, sharp-lighted in the red glare, worked frantically to seal the underground powder magazines against the advancing flames.

A party of half-clad cavaliers appeared, escorting the Queen, the Princesses, and the young Prince toward the far border of the camp. The Queen looked anything but regal now—barefoot, her hair unbound and a cloak gathered askew about her shoulders. But she had control of herself, and Pedro noted that she was carrying a dispatch case. Even at such a time, her first thought had been of irreplaceable official documents. Some distance away he saw the King, on horseback, a half-buckled cuirass on his otherwise bare torso, controling his mount with difficulty as he shouted orders which were lost in the tumult.

At every moment Pedro expected to hear the war cry of attacking Moors. The same apprehension gripped the entire camp. Amid their feverish efforts men threw anxious glances toward Granada. Officers rode back and forth along the flame-lighted street, and as one passed near Pedro his voice carried briefly above the din.

"Save your weapons, men, above all else! Be ready for an attack!"

It was an ominous possibility. But no sound of battle pierced the uproar which pervaded the camp. If the Moors planned an attack it hadn't yet been launched. If one should come, Pedro thought bitterly, his injury would make him as useless in fighting Moors as in fighting the flames. All he could do was look on.

One of the hospital tents was burning now. Then, almost instantly, another and another. The main tent burst into flame even as the last of the wounded were being evacuated. The helpless men lay on the ground nearby, wrapped in sheets. They were out of reach of the flames, but there was no escaping the rain of sparks and glowing cinders, and some of the sheets quickly began to smolder. Someone pointed frantically toward the huge casks which held the hospital's water supply. Obeying the gesture, orderlies snatched the sheets and dashed to the very wall of the blazing tent to douse them in the casks. Then, unmindful of the burning particles falling on their own bare backs and shoulders, they spread the dripping sheets over the patients to shelter them from the fiery showers. Watching, Pedro felt a sudden new respect for hospital orderlies.

Despite all efforts, the fire continued to spread. The breeze which had been so welcome in the early evening had proved treacherous; it blew in strong gusts, sweeping vast swathes of flame across first one section of the camp, then another. Burning shreds of canvas and brushwood whirled aloft, tossed to and fro in the shifting heat currents, then settled with inanimate perversity upon spots upwind from the fire, starting new blazes in widely separated sections. The scattered fires met and merged into unbroken walls of flame. Here and there giant fountains of sparks spewed up as blazing tent poles collapsed.

The sumptuous marquees in the court precinct had already

been destroyed, but furniture and coffers of belongings were still burning fiercely. Some of the court personnel had followed the Queen to the camp's outskirts, some were still milling about in confusion just outside the precinct. Among them Pedro saw some incongruous figures—a woman whose only garment was a lacy shift, desperately clutching a satin slipper in one hand and a silver comb in the other; a dazed-looking girl carrying a still-lighted night lamp, unthinkingly snatched up as she fled; a young page boy, wearing a cap and not a thread else, running about distractedly in search of more adequate covering.

Again he turned toward Granada, certain that an enemy host lurked in the darkness beyond the flame-lit encampment. He saw teeming activity, but no turbaned enemy. He heard shouting voices, but no Moslem war cry. The Moors still had made no attack. What did it mean? What were they waiting for? His apprehension became tinged with puzzlement. Then a dim hope began to stir.

Canvas and brushwood burned swiftly. Soon the soaring leap of the fire weakened as it began to burn itself out. The solid sheets of flame rifted, dwindling gradually to yellow tongues that crawled and flickered amid seething billows of smoke. Then there were only scattered blazes, and at last these too began to die.

Night was nearly over. The stricken camp waited for dawn.

Daylight brought only a feeble grayness filtering through a heavy curtain of smoke. Pedro looked about dazedly. Charred, smoking wreckage lay everywhere, amid great heaps of embers still bright and pulsing with heat. Men were only vague shapes in the murky vapor, half-seen, as if they too were more vapor than substance. The air, hot and acrid, burned his throat with every breath and stung his eyes.

As he peered into the haze a voice sounded at his elbow so suddenly that he was startled.

"If it's Moors you're looking for, you can stop looking."

Pedro swung around and saw the knobby man, still clad only in his ragged breeches.

"There'll be no attack." The little man's voice was dry and rasping from the fumes. "I've been over to the edge of camp, watching the city. Heh! Not a turban stirring."

Pedro's quick relief was mingled with bewilderment. "But why did they start this fire if they didn't intend to attack?"

The man thoughtfully scratched the bump which served him for a chin. "Maybe they didn't start it."

That possibility hadn't even occurred to Pedro. "But—but if they didn't start it, who did?"

"Don't ask me. I haven't the slightest idea." The knobby shoulders hitched upward in a puzzled little shrug.

"Santos!" Pedro stared through the haze in the direction of Granada. "In all that confusion they could have mowed us down like grass."

"Oh, no, they couldn't. Not with three thousand cavalry-men in the way."

"What zhree zhousand cazalrynen?" The stout man had joined them. Swathed in a sheet whose edges trailed on the ground, his head a shapeless white mass of bandages, he looked like a ghostly apparition in the swirling smoke.

"The Marquis de Cádiz's troopers. Well-trained, those lads

—they dashed into action before the fire was scarcely started. Rode out of camp with their swords waving and their armor shining." He gave a little chuckle. The smoke changed it to a cough. "Armor, did I say? Heh! Not a man wearing more than a breastplate. Some only a baldric. Maybe a morion here and there. But that firelight was tricky. It made them flicker and flash as if they were armored from hair to heel. The Moors took one look, and decided they'd be safer behind their walls."

The stout man shook his bandaged head doubtfully. "Zhose Noors don't scare *zhat* easy. Why didn't zhey attack, while ezeryzhing was in such consusion?"

"Thank heaven they didn't, whatever the reason," Pedro said soberly.

Hurried measures were being taken to forestall a belated enemy attack, which even now seemed not unlikely. A huge force of cavalry, in odds and ends of armor salvaged from the ashes, joined the troops of the Marquis de Cádiz between the camp and the city. It was a deceptive show of strength, designed to camouflage the Spaniards' vulnerable state. Perhaps it deceived the Moors, or perhaps their defeat in the parkland had left them incapable of further battle. They made no move. Overwhelming relief swept the camp. The night's disaster had staggered the Spanish forces; an assault at this time might have crushed them.

Faces blanched as the full extent of the havoc became apparent. The camp was a vast shambles. Tents, barracks, provisions, clothing, equipment of every kind had been destroyed. The few spots which had escaped the holocaust seemed to accentuate the general devastation.

The Queen's Hospital was a mass of smoking debris. Wounded men sat or lay on the ground. Surgeons and orderlies moved here and there, doing what little they could for the suffering men. New arrivals, nursing burns and other injuries, were coming in a steady trickle from all sections of the camp. By some incomprehensible miracle, the fire had caused no fatalities, but nearly everyone had suffered minor burns, and some were enduring agonies, with flesh horribly seared. Worst of all, there was no relief for them—the hospital's supplies of balms and bandages had gone up in smoke, or lay buried in the wreckage.

One thing had become clear by now—the Moors hadn't started the fire. But who, then, had? That question was on every tongue. The answer came soon, from the Queen herself, and was known throughout the army within an hour. The devastating blaze had originated in the Queen's pavilion.

It seemed that Her Highness had sat up late the night before, writing dispatches. Upon retiring, she found her rest disturbed by the light from her bedside lamp, and directed that it be moved farther away. One of her ladies-in-waiting moved the lamp to a nearby table, where a drapery shaded its light from the Queen's eyes. The lady-in-waiting was careless. She placed the lamp quite close to the drapery. The breeze —that fateful breeze which the sweltering patients had welcomed so gratefully—swept through the pavilion's upraised canvas walls and set the drapery swaying. The hanging was of fine silk—fine but flimsy, and certainly easily inflammable. . . .

"So *zhat's* how it hattened! Oz all zhe scatter-drained,

stutid . . . !" The stout man stopped, at a loss for adequate words.

His knobby friend responded with a philosophic shrug and a thin grin. "We'll have to give that lady-in-waiting credit for one thing. Heh! She nearly succeeded in doing what all the Moors in Granada couldn't do—destroying the whole Spanish army!"

Pedro shook his head puzzledly. "I still can't understand why the Moors didn't take advantage of the fire to attack the camp."

"Everybody is wondering the same thing," the little man said. "The general opinion is that they thought the whole business was a trick—that we deliberately lit bonfires so as to draw them out of the city. When they saw the Marquis's troopers ride out into the vega, they doubtless thought the rest of us were lying low in the camp, ready to pounce if they should rise to the bait."

"Zhat seens sar-setched."

"Maybe. But there's no other explanation. Now that it's daylight they can see their mistake, of course. Heh! It's enough to make the heathens rip their turbans, seeing what a chance they missed."

The dazed army turned determinedly to the work of salvage and restoration. The Queen, always a woman of action, already had taken steps toward that end. Even as the flames died, her messengers were galloping off toward scores of towns and fortresses with word of what had happened. Every town was directed to send relief supplies at once—food, clothing, tents, medicaments, and other necessities.

There was hunger in the camp that first day. Meager

rations were doled out from the few provisions spared by the
fire. Clothing too was a pressing need. Routed from sleep in
the dead of night, most of the troops were near naked. They
found a grain of gleeful satisfaction in one thing: the officers
and grandees were as destitute of covering as they themselves.

"Don Ferdinand was left with nothing to wear but his
armor. Heh! His armor wouldn't burn." The knobby man's
injury didn't affect his legs, which carried him all over the
camp and brought him back with word of what was happening in various sections. "His Highness had to borrow some
clothes from one of his guardsmen."

"So now what's the guardsman wearing?" Pedro wondered
with a half-hearted attempt at a grin.

"No more than we are, probably. Oh, and doña Isabella's
wardrobe was destroyed too. All those silks and velvets are
nothing but ashes now. What a shame! Heh!" The little
man's tone sounded anything but sympathetic.

Pedro shrugged his indifference to the clothing problems
of the King and Queen. He himself was wearing only his
bandage and his sheet.

He was hobbling about much of the time, too miserable to
remain still, though every step cost his injured leg a painful
throb. But he forgot his own pain at the sight of the suffering
around him. Men lay about on the bare ground, moaning,
sometimes crying out. One could only look on helplessly.
Pedro could have cried like a baby for sheer pity.

But toward nightfall relief supplies began to arrive, and
before the next morning a steady parade of pack animals,
driven unsparingly through the night, was moving into the

camp. The worst was over. A great wave of thankfulness swept the waiting army.

As fast as the supplies arrived they were put to use. There were pallets now for some of the wounded, and bandages and healing ointments for all. There was almost enough to eat again. But the destitute multitude couldn't be provided for in a day. Clothing was still a problem. It was arriving in huge quantities, but of course the nobles were supplied first, and then their elite regiments, and last of all the rank and file. But everybody got at least enough to make do for the time being—a shirt to one man, a tunic to another, hose or breeches to a third. The hospital patients were better served than most. Pedro gratefully discarded his sheet and got into new breeches and shirt, which was all he usually wore in July anyway. His spirits lifted at once, as if he had put on new courage along with the new clothes.

But there was a flaw in his satisfaction. His seaman's stocking-cap was gone. Whether lost during the battle or destroyed in the fire he didn't know, but in either case it was gone. It had been a symbol, that cap, with its salty suggestion of ships and seafarers. Wearing it, Pedro could imagine himself already the sailor he planned to become. Without it, he felt almost shorn of identity. A mere nobody. A—a *landsman!*

The army wasn't alone in being newly outfitted—so reported the knobby man, who had been out gathering more news.

"The Queen has a whole new wardrobe, thanks to Gonzalo de Córdova's wife. Don Gonzalo sent word of the fire to his castle in Illora, and when his wife heard how the Queen's

entire wardrobe had been destroyed, she sent *her* entire
wardrobe here to replace it."

"How zery generous!" The stout man's muffled voice was
heavy with sarcasm.

"And how very smart! Don Gonzalo's wife knows how to
help her husband's career."

The Queen not only had a new wardrobe, the little man
went on. She also had a new tent—the largest and finest of
the many being brought to the camp. It had already been set
up, just outside the ruined campground, and would serve as
temporary quarters for Her Highness and her ladies-in-
waiting.

"It's big and it's fancy," he summed up, "but it can't
compare with that gorgeous pavilion she had before."

Pedro chuckled. "I'll wager there'll be no silk draperies
hung in this one."

For the most part, an air of dogged courage prevailed in
the camp. Men labored tirelessly, unpacking supplies, clearing away wreckage, sifting through ashes to reclaim still-
usable articles. But the loss had been staggering, and there
were those who wondered if the siege could be maintained.
There was talk of suspending operations until the following
spring, to allow an interval for recovery. It was rumored that
the Sovereigns were conferring with their advisors, debating
what should be done.

Decision came swiftly. It was relayed to the various units
by their captains, but the hospital patients were privileged to
hear it from the Queen's own lips. She visited them un-
announced, escorted by a small group of cavaliers. Her face
went soft with commiseration as she looked at the injured

men. They watched her, held in an expectant hush, waiting for her to speak.

Her voice was tense but firm, and she came to the point at once.

"Doubts have been raised that we can survive the calamity which God has seen fit to allow. There are ample reasons for the doubts. Our possessions lie about us in ashes. Our camp is destroyed. So be it. We shall not set up another."

There was a rustle of astonished protest at the implication of the words. It was stilled at once as the Queen raised her hand for silence and went on.

"No, we will not rebuild the camp. We will do better. We will build a city in its place. Not a collection of temporary barracks, but permanent buildings of brick and stone. Not an array of flimsy tents which can be destroyed in a moment, but a city that will endure through years and centuries to come—as long as yonder city of Granada shall endure. Thus will our enemies see how strong is our purpose, how steadfast our faith, how futile their resistance."

She paused. The silence was deep and wondering, the import of her words too amazing to be grasped quickly. After a moment she spoke on, and there was a prophetic ring in her voice.

"Here we stand at the gates of Granada. Here we shall stay until those gates open to admit our banners—until the Christian Cross supplants the Moslem Crescent upon Granada's towers."

Her words rang out across the blackened campground like victory bells. Could they be heard in Granada, Pedro thought, they would sound more like a death knell.

Happy News

Pedro grasped the handles of the wheelbarrow, lifted it, then set it back down. That load of tiles was heavier than it looked. He removed the topmost two or three and put them back on the stack where he'd got them. Then he gripped the handles again, straightened, and shoved off, the wheelbarrow creaking in loud complaint at being compelled to carry such a load.

Pedro's eyes flicked here and there as he moved along, only vaguely noticing the busy scene around him, for it had become familiar by now. Familiar, yet always changing, always a little different with each passing day. Who'd think that only a few weeks ago this place had been a waste of smoking ashes! Just look at it now! It looked like—like . . . . Well, certainly not like an army encampment. It was about as military-looking as a barnyard at feeding time.

Soldiers had turned builders. Weapons had been traded for tools. On every hand was teeming activity. Men clambered about scaffolding, climbed and descended ladders, mixed mortar, chiseled stone, nailed up rafters, sawed planks. Great cranes and pulleys raised heavy stones into place upon half-finished walls. Architects and engineers, brought from all over Spain, scanned scale-drawings and made careful checks with plumb lines and levels.

The men of the provincial units had turned eagerly to the work of construction. Until recently nearly all had been civilians, and nearly all were skilled at some craft or other, at least passably so. And there were tasks for unskilled men as well—Pedro could attest to that. He was doing a full share of the work, for his wound was all but healed now, save for a livid scar, an almost unnoticed ache, and a slight limp.

He wove his wheelbarrow among a variety of obstacles— trestles and tool boxes, piles of stone and lumber, workmen pushing barrows or carrying hods or dragging handcarts. He swerved aside as he met an ox-drawn cartload of building stones, headed in the opposite direction. As it lumbered past, shaking up a gritty cloud from its dust-powdered bed, a particle lodged in Pedro's eye. He blinked ineffectually, then lowered the wheelbarrow, which gave a relieved squeak as it came to rest. While he stood knuckling his eye, Paco's voice sounded from close at hand.

"What's the matter, Pedro?" There was more banter than concern in the question. "Working too hard? Wheelbarrow too heavy?"

Pedro cleared his eye before answering. "The wheelbarrow's light enough. What bothers me is the load that's on it." Still blinking, he turned toward Paco. "What about *you*? On holiday?"

Paco was idle at the moment, but he and a partner stood by a great drum windlass, waiting for the signal to start turning it again. Paco's long, strong arms were made to order for turning drum windlasses. He grinned. "Holiday, is it? *Madre mia!* I'm breaking my back at this windlass to make sure the Galicians don't beat us in the building race." Men of the various provinces were competing to be the first to complete their assigned sections of the project.

"You're not breaking your back fast enough," Pedro told him. "The Galicians are still ahead, and the Valencians aren't far behind. We're going to have to stir ourselves if we hope to finish first."

"Don't worry, we'll finish first," Paco said confidently.

"That we will," his partner agreed. "Andalusians take second place to no one. All we need is—"

A shout from overhead interrupted him. "Ready! Hoist away!"

Paco and his partner stopped talking and grasped the windlass spokes. Their muscles strained as they turned the great cylinder, hauling a heavy stone aloft by means of block and tackle attached to a tall wooden derrick. Pedro watched in fascination. There is something about a derrick that fascinates a spectator, in any country, in any century. However, his own task was waiting, and he lingered only briefly. He and the wheelbarrow moved on, Pedro puffing a bit, the wheelbarrow wobbling under its burden.

Pedro halted by a scaffolded wall, atop which masons were laying a final row of stone before starting on the roof. Before unloading the tiles, he reached for the water flask at his belt. It was thirsty work, pushing a wheelbarrow under this late August sun. Over the up-tilted flask, he looked past his busy surroundings to the red-walled city on the mountain skirts.

Not a shadow of activity showed there. Granada had made no move since the day of the battle in the parkland, well over a month ago. Those parties of horsemen who used to harass the camp's borders never appeared any more. Not a figure ever showed itself outside the city's walls. Of course, the Spaniards were taking no chances. While the rank and file labored, the crack troops kept up their normal practice at arms, and a regiment was still kept always alert, ready to spring to battle should the need arise. But no one expected that the need would arise. The Moors apparently had no fight left in them.

Pedro hung his flask back at his belt and started unloading the tiles, working mechanically, his thoughts on other things. Andrés, he remembered, had predicted that the fighting was over when the work of construction first started.

"This kills the heathens' last hope," Andrés had declared, sounding as glum as if it were his own last hope that was being killed. "They know now that we're here to stay, and there's nothing they can do except surrender—or else starve." Then his sad voice took on an almost cheerful note as he added, "Building this city will end the war more surely than winning a dozen battles."

Most of the other veteran soldiers held the same opinion. Oh, everybody had been jittery for a while, right after the fire, feeling sure that the Moors would take advantage of the situation and launch an attack. But Granada had remained shut up as against a plague, and before long the men had stopped worrying about the Moorish city. They had plenty to occupy their minds and hands, building a city of their own.

The soldiers welcomed the work. The constant activity left no time for looking back, no time for sadness. The comrades who had shared The Nest seldom spoke of Marcos. Had the shelter not been destroyed, the big man's personality would have clung to the place like a living presence. As it was, every reminder was gone, and though they remembered him with affection, the poignant sense of loss was dulled.

Pedro thought often of Felipe. His first bitterness toward the man had passed; he realized now that it had been unjustified. Felipe hadn't acted treacherously—warning one's countrymen of danger isn't treachery. The act was to be admired, not condemned. Pedro knew now that he had lost nothing of his liking and respect for Felipe. When the war was over, should they by some remote chance meet again, it would be as friends. Friendship between Spaniard and Moor wasn't unheard of—he thought of Gonzalo de Córdova and Boabdil. It was a comforting thought.

The wheelbarrow was empty now, the tiles laid in a neat row on the stack, waiting for the roofers. He straightened and flicked away a drop of sweat that was tickling his nose. Not far away he saw Chico scuttling up a ladder, carrying a mallet up to a workman on a scaffold. Pedro smiled at the sight. Chico, short and light and totally without nerves, could scurry about on scaffoldings and narrow beams like a squirrel on high branches.

Pedro started back for another load of tiles, the wheelbarrow bouncing along ahead, giving happy little squeaks of relief at being rid of its burden. Again he came to the windlass where Paco was working, again during a momentary interval of idleness. He threw Paco a look of mock disapproval.

"Do you spend all your time leaning against that wheel? No wonder we're behind in the building race!"

"Look who's talking!" Paco called back. "If you *must* keep rambling around with that wheelbarrow, you might at least put something in it." Suddenly he dropped his bantering manner and motioned toward a point beyond Pedro. "There's doña Isabella again. Doesn't she ever rest?"

Pedro's eyes followed Paco's gesture. Some distance away he saw doña Isabella, studying a sheet of plans an architect was showing her. Pedro turned back to Paco.

"Nobody rests these days. Not even the Queen."

A few weeks ago the sight of the Queen would have caused a stir of excitement, but now doña Isabella had become a familiar figure to the workers. She was everywhere, eagerly watching the progress, encouraging the builders, inspecting materials, consulting with architects and engineers. And it was said that she examined drawings and diagrams by lamplight, far into each night, going over the plans for her city.

For this was the Queen's city—that was common knowledge. Who but doña Isabella could have envisioned such a project? Not don Ferdinand, certainly. Don Ferdinand was brave in battle, shrewd and wily in politics, but his worldly-wise mind could never have conceived a project such as this. To build a city in order to lay siege to a city! The boldness of the plan had made the whole army gasp. Yet somehow no one doubted that it was bound to succeed.

Paco's partner spoke. "The Queen has her work to do. We have ours."

Confirming the statement, a shouted signal came from overhead. "Ready! Hoist away!"

Pedro had already started off, but he couldn't resist lingering a moment longer to watch the derrick operate. In an unthinking gesture, still habitual after more than a month, he lifted his hand to push his stocking-cap to the back of his head. Instead of the cap, his hand encountered the conventional kerchief which had replaced it. The kerchief was gay in color, light in weight, certainly more comfortable in this sultry weather than the woolen cap. But Pedro felt a mild irritation. He still preferred the cap.

For only a moment he watched the derrick, then he dutifully moved on. Back where the supply of tiles was stacked he grounded the wheelbarrow and began to reload.

The hot August days drew on toward September. The city continued to grow. Walls rose higher, acquired roofs, took shape as houses and public buildings. Defensive stone bulwarks enclosed the city, complete with watch towers and battlements. Two broad paved avenues formed the principal thoroughfares, intersecting at the central plaza. At the left of the plaza a church was erected, and just opposite, the buildings which were to serve as the royal headquarters.

Priority had been given to completing this section, and already the Sovereigns had taken up residence there. They and their court were housed in barely-completed structures, surrounded by the noise and bustle of construction still in progress. The grandees and officers were living in tents, set up just outside the ruined camp site. The common soldiers did without shelter. In this season little or no rain fell, and the sky was shelter enough. They slept in the open, wherever they could find a space amid the clutter of construction.

"I could sleep on a pile of gravel, I'm that tired," Paco complained at the end of one arduous day. "Ay, my back! It's tied in knots all the way down my spine."

"With such a long spine, that could be serious," Pedro quipped unfeelingly.

Chico said, "I'm glad I'm short. There's less of me to get tired."

The evening meal was over, and the men had moved away from the embers of the cooking fires to seek relatively cool spots. Night had closed in, but the moon hung like a big yellow orange in a sky pin-pointed with stars, lighting the world with a glow that was almost as revealing as daylight. From all around the sounds of voices rose and ebbed, with a lighthearted laugh or an ill-humored growl breaking in from time to time. In a nearby group, shouted banter and a brief scuffle indicated that someone still had energy enough for a bit of horseplay.

"One good thing, we don't have to stand sentry duty," Pedro observed. "I'd rather push a wheelbarrow any day than walk sentry duty."

"Or go through arms drills," Chico added.

"Or stand battle watch with the duty regiment." Paco rested his elbows on his knees and his chin on his knuckles. "I don't envy those trained troops, sweating in their stuffy armor, waiting for a battle that's never coming."

"What makes you so sure it isn't?"

"*Caramba!* The Moors certainly aren't showing any signs of attacking."

"They aren't showing any signs of surrendering, either," Pedro said. "But I won't argue about it, because I think you're right, for once."

"Thanks. Not that it matters what you think."

The trio suddenly stopped talking. Somewhere amid the

surrounding babble a rich clear voice rose in song. The song
was one of the region's traditional ballads, which invariably
told of love unrequited, or love thwarted, or love passed
away; and it was sung in the region's traditional manner, the
notes soaring high, floating in a succession of trills, then
fading almost to silence before rising again. The singer wove
a spell in the night. Conversation hushed; men listened with
dreamy expressions, plunged into a mood of nostalgia, their
thoughts turning to homes and families and their sweethearts.

Pedro caught the spell. He sat with hands clasped over
updrawn knees, shoulders swaying slightly in rhythm with
the song's slow measure. He too was indulging in memories
of home—the only home he had ever known. La Rábida was
far away, but he could picture the place as clearly as if he
were there at this moment. He thought fondly of young
Diego and his other classmates and companions. He called
the various monks to mind. Their dark-robed figures, once so
familiar a part of his life, seemed as real to his vivid imagination as the men around him.

Suddenly Pedro sat up straighter and stared. Sentimental
fancies went flying out of his mind like startled sparrows.
That approaching figure in the Franciscan habit was no
figment of imagination. It was quite material—and strangely
familiar. A tall, slender monk was moving from group to
group, obviously searching for someone. As he turned toward
the spot where Pedro sat the moonlight fell full upon his
face—a striking face, both strong and sensitive, lined by years
yet somehow youthful-looking.

For an instant Pedro stared in unbelief. Then he gave a

little yelp, sprang to his feet, and bounded forward, heedless of his not-quite-mended leg.

"*Fray Juan!*"

The monk's face broke into a joyous smile. "*Pedro!*" He clasped the youth in a fatherly embrace, then stood back and beamed. "Pedro! How good it is to see you! I do believe you've grown taller. Sturdier, too. Army life must agree with you."

Pedro's emotions were a mixture of delight, surprise, and sheer incredulity. "I—I just can't believe my eyes!" He shook his head in happy bewilderment. "What in the world brought you all the way from La Rábida?"

Fray Juan's eyes twinkled. "A mule brought me, naturally. It would have been a long journey to make on foot—though I've surely walked the same distance since I arrived, searching for you."

"How did you ever find me in a place like this?"

"It wasn't easy. The master-at-arms consulted his muster lists and directed me to this section of the camp. After that it was a matter of patient searching."

Pedro, still happily dazed, got hold of himself and swept a quick look about. "You must be bone-tired. Come, Fray Juan—let's find a spot where we can sit and talk."

"I'll admit to being tired. And I'm more than eager for a talk." As they moved away the monk's tone took on a note of concern. "You're limping. You've been hurt?"

"It's nothing—just a scratch that's nearly healed." A sudden uneasiness smote Pedro. Only something unusual could account for the friar's presence here. "How are you, Fray Juan? And Diego? And—and all the others?"

"We all enjoy our usual health—or at least endure it," the friar said cheerfully. "By the way, Diego sends his regards, and says he misses you."

"I miss him, too. I've missed everybody." Pedro indicated a stack of timbers and they sank down side by side. His curiosity overflowed. "What's happened, Fray Juan, that could bring you all this distance? Something very important, surely?"

"Important? Yes, I should call it important. Nothing less than a summons from the Queen." Pedro's eyes bugged, and the friar's smile broadened. "I knew you'd be interested—it concerns a very special friend of yours."

Pedro guessed at once whom he meant. "Captain Columbus!"

"Of course, Captain Columbus." Fray Juan's manner suddenly seemed less cheerful. "He is at La Rábida now, though it took all my powers of persuasion to keep him from setting out for France."

"France!"

The friar nodded gravely. "He had made up his mind to leave Spain and seek backing for the Enterprise at the French court." Then, seeing Pedro's dismayed expression, he went on quickly. "However, he has changed his intention, thank heaven, at least for the time being."

Pedro's silence was eloquent with anxious questions. Fray Juan proceeded to answer them.

"Captain Columbus came to La Rábida to get Diego—he had decided to leave the boy with relatives in Huelva during his stay in France. He was bitter about his wasted years in Spain, and intended to leave without delay." The monk shook his head slowly and soberly. "His feelings were under-standable, certainly. Six years of frustration and disappoint-ment! Most men would have given up long ago. However, I begged him to reconsider. Let us try once more, I urged him. Let me write personally to the Queen and ask her to give the case another hearing. At first he refused unequivocally. He'd been waiting for six years, he told me—now he was through with waiting. But finally I persuaded him to put off his de-parture at least long enough for me to send Her Highness a letter and get a reply. Luckily, I have her ear—she and I have long been friends."

Pedro nodded. "I know. She told me."

Fray Juan turned and stared. "She told you! You've talked with doña Isabella?"

"Yes." Despite his eagerness to hear the story, Pedro couldn't resist dramatizing a bit. "Oh, by the way, Her High-ness spoke about you, Fray Juan. She said you are often in her thoughts." He enjoyed the other's amazement briefly, then impatience got the better of him. "Actually, doña Isa-bella just spoke a few words to me while she was visiting the hospital. But about the letter . . . ?"

The friar, still surprised, seemed to grope for the thread of his story.

"Ah, yes—the letter. Well, I wrote it without delay, and Sebastián Rodríguez agreed to carry it to the Queen. Se-bastián is a boat pilot, but he welcomes a courier's assign-ment whenever one presents itself. He made the journey with all speed, and within two weeks was back at the monas-tery with the Queen's reply. Believe me, Pedro, never have I received happier news. Doña Isabella wrote me to come to

the camp and discuss the matter with her in person. Columbus, meanwhile, she bade remain at La Rábida and await her
summons—which, she assured him, would be forthcoming
shortly.

"It goes without saying that I wasted no time. I borrowed
a mule from the Pinzón brothers and left La Rábida in all
haste." Fray Juan chuckled. "Unfortunately, the mule wasn't
in nearly as much of a hurry as I was—I'm sure the obstinate
beast could have cut a day off the journey with just a bit of
good will. At any rate, I finally arrived this morning, and
spent most of the afternoon with doña Isabella."

"And . . . ?" Pedro prompted eagerly.

"And doña Isabella has decided to send for Columbus at
once."

Pedro uttered a wordless sound of elation, a kind of joyful
gurgle.

"Also," Fray Juan continued, "she is going to send him
money to buy a mount for the trip and clothe himself fittingly for an audience. You know how poorly he has to dress
—for all his pride, he can't hide his poverty. It needed only a
hint from me that his threadbare doublet was scarcely appro-
priate for a court appearance, and Her Highness was quick to
make adequate provision."

Pedro smacked his palms together in excitement. "Surely
doña Isabella intends to finance the Enterprise—else she
wouldn't have sent for him."

The friar nodded thoughtfully. "There is no doubt of her
interest—she has made it quite plain. However, I doubt if
anything definite will be decided until the Moors are defeated."

"That will be soon!" Pedro's voice trilled like a songbird.

A rush of joyous thoughts whisked through his mind in a mere tick of time. So he'd plotted his course correctly, after all! It had been a wise decision, choosing the army instead of the sea. It had placed him where he'd meet Captain Columbus. And he'd be right at hand for the long-awaited approval of the Enterprise. Exactly as he'd planned! Smart lad, Pedro!

He leaned forward eagerly. "How long will it be before Captain Columbus gets here?"

The other calculated. "Let me see—allow time for the Queen's letter to reach La Rábida, and then for Columbus to make his purchases and prepare for the journey, and add the time he'll be on the road. All in all, I'd say he should arrive in about two weeks, give or take a day or so."

"That's going to be the longest two weeks I've ever spent. I can hardly wait."

Fray Juan's eyes twinkled like altar candles. "Neither can Captain Columbus."

Class Barriers

Following Fray Juan's visit, Pedro's emotions kept swinging like a pendulum. One minute he was bubbling with excitement, the next lost in daydreams. It almost surprised him to see everyone else behaving as usual. He had to keep reminding himself that they didn't know Captain Columbus was coming, and wouldn't be interested if they did.

His talk with Fray Juan hadn't gone unnoticed, of course, and his comrades showed a natural curiosity. Pedro eagerly explained who the friar was, but said nothing of the thrilling news he had brought, though it was burning the tip of his tongue. Wary of scornful comments about his idol, he was still carefully avoiding any mention of Columbus and the Enterprise.

But though Pedro could control his tongue, his face could never keep a secret. A few days after Fray Juan's visit, as Pedro finished supper and moved away from the fire, Paco skewered a slab of sausage on his knife and moved off beside him. Paco was eying him quizzically, but he didn't speak until they settled themselves a little apart from the others.

"He must have brought you quite a piece of news, Pedro."

Pedro looked blank. "He? Who?"

" 'He-who,' " Paco mocked. "The friar—that's he-who.

This Fray Juan of yours. Ever since you saw him, you've been either lit up like a lantern or lost in a cloud. I'd never dream of asking a nosy question—but what in the world did he tell you?"

Pedro frowned. It was disconcerting to realize how transparent he'd been. He tried to brush off the question with a shrug.

Paco responded with a shrug of his own, elaborately casual. "It isn't that I'm curious. It's just that I'm itching to find out." Then his gaze sharpened. "I'll stake this hunk of sausage that it had something to do with your sailor friend. Columbus, I believe you called him."

Pedro blinked. "How—how did you know?"

"*Hombre!* If it was anything else you wouldn't be trying to hide it." Paco snickered. "You haven't a chance, Pedro. The more you try to keep something to yourself, the more it shows all over you." He bit into the sausage and munched appreciatively, his eyes still mocking.

Ay! Pedro thought. Paco couldn't read a written page, but how he could read faces! Might as well tell him what he already guessed.

"It was news, all right," he began, then stopped and flicked a wary glance around. But the others were intent on their supper or on their own conversation, so he went on. "I've got reason to be excited. Captain Columbus is coming."

"So is doomsday. But I knew it was something of the sort. Nothing else could make you look so moon-struck—unless you'd fallen in love." Suddenly Paco lost his bantering manner and eyed Pedro in frank puzzlement. "You know, Pedro, it's beyond me how you can be taken in by that man's absurd ideas. On other matters you show a fair amount of sense." His obvious sincerity smoothed the rude edge from the words; Paco was genuinely puzzled, unable to understand.

Pedro shook his head helplessly. How could he defend Captain Columbus against such invincible disbelief?

A little frown puckered Paco's forehead. "I know that you like the man, but that's no reason to go along with everything he says." His air of patient remonstrance would have been exasperating if it weren't so earnest. "Surely you don't *really* believe in his fantastic scheme!"

Pedro had a sudden inspiration. "It seems that doña Isabella believes in his 'fanastic scheme'—else she wouldn't have sent for him."

"What do you mean, sent for him?"

"Just what I say. Doña Isabella wrote Captain Columbus a personal letter, summoning him to the court to discuss the Enterprise. What's more, she provided him with funds to get here." He shot Paco a triumphant look. "Come now, Paco. The Queen takes his ideas seriously—surely you don't question *her* good sense!"

It was a telling shot. Paco's bony jaw dropped. He looked almost panicky, as if he'd just stepped off solid ground into a gaping void. He lowered his sausage and searched desperately for a hole in Pedro's argument. But it seemed quite holeproof—one could hardly call Columbus a lunatic if the Queen herself believed in him. As Pedro gloated over his discomfiture, Rodrigo's quiet voice sounded.

"What's all this about doña Isabella? And who is Captain

Columbus?" Rodrigo had come up unnoticed and had evidently caught a part of their conversation.

Pedro hesitated, then realized with a flash of elation that it was safe to speak freely. The argument which had quelled Paco would be just as effective against any other scoffer. Swiftly, his voice low but eager, he gave Rodrigo the main facts about Columbus and the Enterprise. Rodrigo listened with interest. He apparently saw nothing startling in the idea of a round earth, but Paco voiced another weak protest.

"So the world's round, like an oversized orange!" He turned to Rodrigo, hoping for support. "Can you imagine anyone believing such nonsense?"

"Wiser men than I seem to believe it," Rodrigo said noncommittally.

Paco growled something unintelligible and fell silent, finishing his sausage with no sign of relish. Pedro sat watching him, wearing a smug expression. Then he noticed that Rodrigo too was silent, his blue eyes thoughtful. Suddenly Rodrigo turned to him.

"This Fray Juan must be a very persuasive letter writer, Pedro. You say that Columbus has presented his case at court several times, that scholars and statesmen have studied it and turned him down, that he has been kept dangling for six years. And now a letter from a friar suddenly stirs up the Queen's interest—with a war on her mind, at that—so much so that she immediately summons both Fray Juan and Columbus to court!" He shook his head in puzzlement. "I'd be interested in knowing just what Fray Juan wrote in that letter."

Pedro reflected for an interval before responding. He too had wondered why that letter should have caused such an impression on doña Isabella. Surely there was more in it than a request that Captain Columbus be given another hearing, for after all, the matter had been thoroughly threshed out again and again. Had some new factor arisen in the case? Had Captain Columbus produced fresh evidence in support of his theories, or perhaps revealed clues to Fray Juan which for some reason he had thus far kept to himself? Who could know? There were questions which only Fray Juan, doña Isabella, and Captain Columbus could answer.

Pedro spoke thoughtfully. "It's a big question, Rodrigo. But whatever it was that Fray Juan wrote, it brought results. That's what really matters."

But Pedro was to ponder the question often and fruitlessly for as long as he lived. And, though he couldn't even suspect it, men then unborn would be wondering about that letter's contents in years and centuries yet to come.

The busy days sped by, Pedro counting them off in eager anticipation. Fray Juan sought him out again one evening and they enjoyed another chat. Fray Juan promised to let him know without delay when Columbus arrived—"the moment he dismounts," the friar added with a smile. To Pedro, never had the world seemed a finer place. Captain Columbus was coming, and the Enterprise would soon be launched, and he could at last talk all he pleased about his idol and his dream. And just let anyone dare lift a mocking eyebrow, now that the Queen herself was involved!

Strangely enough, now that he could speak of the subject

freely, he didn't overdo it. He told Chico that Columbus was coming, and got a matter-of-fact, "That's nice," in response. When he mentioned it to Rodrigo, he met friendly interest, but no keen enthusiasm. With Paco, Pedro was careful to talk of other matters.

Poor Paco! He was still completely bewildered. His own eyes told him that the world is flat. Nothing could be more obvious. Yet many supposedly rational people, including the Queen herself, maintained that it is round. It just didn't make sense to Paco. Why, one might as well go a step further and claim that the sun doesn't circle around the earth!

Pedro smiled inwardly at Paco's discomfiture, but he was generous enough not to gloat. He'd won his point, and a winner can afford to be generous.

He hummed happily to himself one afternoon as he dumped a barrowful of wood chips onto a trash pile to be burned. Then, still humming, he started back for another load, the empty wheelbarrow rolling along ahead with skittish little bounces. Suddenly, hearing his name called, he stopped and looked around. A man of his unit was pointing him out to one of the camp waterboys, who had come up with his laden burro.

"Over here, Pedro!" the man called. "This lad is looking for you."

What now? Pedro thought. He put the wheelbarrow down and started toward the two, hoping he wasn't in any trouble with the head sergeant. The waterboy came to meet him halfway, looking at him uncertainly.

"Is your name—ah—Pedro Tegero?"

"It sure is." Pedro searched his memory uneasily for something he might have done or left undone.

"The Pedro Tegero from a place called—ah—" The boy looked worried, then relieved. "Oh, yes—La Rábida."

Pedro's heart gave an expectant skip. "That's me."

"Then I guess you're the Pedro Tegero I'm supposed to give this message to. A friar sent me, from over by the court precinct. He said to tell you—ah—" The boy's forehead screwed into an intent pucker. Pedro held his breath. "Oh, yes! He said, 'Our friend has arrived.'"

Pedro expelled his breath in an ecstatic whoof. The boy's head bobbed up and down emphatically. "Yes, that was it. 'Our friend has arrived.'" He beamed, looking proud at having fulfilled his mission so competently. "That's all the friar said."

"That's all he needed to say!" With jubilant extravagance, Pedro upended his wallet and dumped its entire contents—a few coppers—into the messenger's waiting palm. It must have been more than the boy expected, for his smile spread all over his face. He moved off, leading his burro, his shrill voice piercing the surrounding din.

"Ah-h—guah-h-h! Ah-h—guah-h-h!"

Pedro, his wallet empty but his heart filled with joy, turned back to his waiting wheelbarrow. So Captain Columbus was here at last! Doubtless he and Fray Juan were discussing the Enterprise with doña Isabella at this moment. Pedro felt a wave of affection for the kindly friar, who even amid such urgent business had remembered to send him the news.

As the first thrill subsided, he began to consider something he had scarcely thought of before. How could he contrive to see Captain Columbus, now that he was here? Captain Columbus was unlikely to seek him out as Fray Juan had done—he had far more important matters on his mind than a meeting with a young friend of his son. Pedro would be satisfied with just a few minutes' chat, but even that wouldn't be easy to arrange. Columbus would never be far from the court, and the court precinct was forbidden ground to a common soldier. The fact stopped Pedro like a solid wall.

For the rest of the afternoon he pondered as he worked. He was still pondering after supper that evening, as he set out alone toward the central plaza. He had no clear idea in mind, other than to approach the court precinct and reconnoiter, hoping some solution would occur to him. The nearer he drew to the forbidden precinct, the larger the problem loomed. Keeping at a respectful distance he scanned the lantern-lighted area. A few figures were moving about, lords and ladies taking the air, but Captain Columbus wasn't among them—and even had he been, Pedro couldn't get within speaking distance.

Presently, still without the foggiest wisp of a plan, he circled around to a narrow street just off the plaza, where the court domestics were quartered. He felt bolder here, and dared to approach closer. Suddenly a brusque voice halted him.

"You, there! Get back to your own section. Who do you think you are, to be hanging around the court precinct!"

It was only an officious lackey, but from his lordly tone he might have been the King himself. The court's household

staff was as class-conscious as the court it served, a ladder of
prestige on which everyone from broom boy to chamberlain
had his own proud rung. For a lowly soldier to intrude into
their domain was nothing less than sacrilege.

Pedro gave up. Slowly he walked back to his unit, meditat-
ing glumly on the unfairness of the social structure. Captain
Columbus was right over there in the court precinct. But for
all the good it did Pedro, he might as well be in the Indies.

Pedro spent the next few days in a ferment of suspense
and impatience. He comforted himself with the knowledge
that Fray Juan would let him know what was developing as
soon as possible. Sure enough, the friar appeared one evening
just after the supper hour. Pedro saw him coming and hurried to meet him, his face alive with eager questions.

Fray Juan began answering them before they could even be
asked. The outlook was encouraging, he told Pedro. The
Queen had decided to appoint a commission to study the
Enterprise and report on its feasibility.

Pedro felt a swift disappointment. "Another commission?
Then there's still no definite decision?"

"Oh, come now, Pedro. These matters take time. But
don't worry—doña Isabella has made it plain that she herself
approves, so we can rest assured that the commission will
follow her lead. Of course, we can expect no final action until
Granada surrenders."

Pedro fetched a faint sigh. Was there no end to waiting?

"The commission is still incomplete, but discussions are
already being held," Fray Juan went on. "Doña Isabella is
choosing its members carefully. They are mariners or schol-

ars, for the most part—men who can appreciate the significance of the Enterprise."

"Do they seem sympathetic to Captain Columbus?"

Fray Juan made a noncommittal gesture. "Most of them disagree with him strongly in their ideas about this earth we live on."

Pedro looked at him in surprise. "Surely there's no argument about the earth being round?"

"No, no, of course not. The point in question isn't the earth's shape, but its size. Columbus maintains that the earth is small—that one can sail to the Indies in a relatively short time. The others claim that the earth is far larger than he believes, and that a westward route to the Indies is impractical because of the vast distance."

"Captain Columbus will prove them wrong," Pedro asserted confidently.

"Um-m-m . . . perhaps." A faraway look came into Fray Juan's eyes. "But suppose Captain Columbus *is* mistaken. Suppose the distance to the Indies is indeed far greater than he imagines. That would mean one of two things—either a vast and unbroken expanse of ocean lies between us and the Indies, or. . . ."

"Or . . . ?" Pedro prompted, as the other paused.

"Or there is land intervening. Islands, perhaps even a continent, as yet unknown." Fray Juan nodded musingly. "It is a possibility, Pedro—a fascinating possibility."

Pedro looked startled. A hitherto unknown continent lying between Spain and the Indies? A fascinating possibility, indeed. But he didn't like such toying with his idol's convictions.

"Captain Columbus isn't mistaken," he insisted.

Fray Juan shot him an amused glance. "Forbid the thought!" he exclaimed with gentle sarcasm. "Sages, saints, and scholars may be mistaken, but never Captain Columbus!"

Pedro grinned sheepishly. But he couldn't bring himself to qualify his view. Captain Columbus mistaken? Impossible!

The two enjoyed only a brief chat, for Fray Juan explained that he couldn't stay long. "Captain Columbus meets tonight with some commission members, and I promised him I'd be on hand. This is quite a busy period, as I'm sure you understand. But I took advantage of this free hour to bring you word of what is happening."

"I'm grateful, Fray Juan. There's no other way I can keep in touch." Pedro fell in beside the friar, to walk back with him as far as the court precinct. He shook his head wistfully. "It's exasperating. For months I've been hoping Captain Columbus would come, and now that he *is* here, I can't even see him."

"Oh, you'll have plenty of leisure as soon as the city is finished, surely."

"That isn't what I meant. If I should dare set foot in the court precinct, I'd be thrown out by the scruff of my neck."

"Ah, I see." The friar's voice took on a satiric note. "Oh, the vanity of men! The humblest of us may freely approach the King of Heaven—He is as close as our own hearts. But the kings of earth, in their petty pride, must set themselves apart." He was silent for a moment, thoughtful. Suddenly he chuckled. "By the way, Pedro, Captain Columbus likes to take a short stroll in the late afternoon. It clears the mind, he

says. Usually he stays close to the court precinct." He gave
Pedro a meaning little nudge. "It occurs to me that if one's
timing is careful, one might be strolling in the same vicinity
at the same hour—by mere chance, to be sure."

Pedro laughed aloud. "You know, Fray Juan, I've a feeling
that I'm going to be strolling there quite often—by mere
chance, to be sure."

Disillusionment

The city was finished. Structures of stone rose where canvas tents and brushwood shelters had stood less than three months before. Formidable walls and battlements replaced the trenches and earthworks which had encircled the camp. In silent challenge, the newly-built city in the plain confronted the centuries-old city on the mountain's skirts.

Now came a flurry of preparations for the solemn dedication. A name for the new city was yet to chosen officially, but the army had already settled that matter to its own satisfaction. Officers and men were one in agreement—the city should of course be named after doña Isabella.

But the Queen declined the compliment.

"Our city was not built to honor an earthly sovereign," she declared. "Let it be dedicated to our Christian Faith, for it is the only city in Spain which has never been touched by Moslem beliefs."

So it was that the new city received the name of Santa Fe —Holy Faith.

The troops were all lodged in substantial quarters now, and none too soon, for the dry summer months were nearly past and the autumn rains could be expected before very long.

Pedro and his former barrackmates shared one of the houses with a few dozen other soldiers. Even among so many, the five maintained much of their former companionship.

"We've lost our privacy," Rodrigo commented, "but we'll still be close friends."

" 'Close' is right," Paco agreed, glancing around the well-packed room. The new quarters were large, but the occupants were many.

The sudden cessation of work left the troops with unaccustomed leisure. There were few tasks to be done, other than caring for quarters and personal gear. Practice at arms, suspended during the busy weeks just past, was resumed in an easy-going fashion, more for the exercise than from any sense of urgency. The fighting was over—there seemed no doubt of that. The army settled down to waiting.

Now at last Pedro could try Fray Juan's suggestion as to how he might meet Columbus. Taking advantage of his freedom, he began haunting the vicinity of the court precinct in the late afternoons. There was considerable territory to watch, since a street led into the area from each of the four sides. They were busy streets too, swarming with people on horseback or afoot.

Pedro knew that Columbus would be glad to see him, but didn't hope for a lengthy talk. After all, the man was intensely busy, dealing with people constantly and with much to weigh on his mind. A solitary stroll might appeal to him far more than a chat with a young hero-worshipper. But just to see his idol, exchange a few pleasant words—that was all Pedro asked.

He was disappointed on the first day, and again on the

second. Undaunted, he came back for a third try. For nearly an hour he wandered about, his eyes searching back and forth constantly but fruitlessly. Suddenly his heart leaped, and he started forward so eagerly that he ran smack into a passer-by. The man gave a startled yelp.

"Cuidado! You careless, witless . . . !" No telling what he might have added had he not, just in time, remembered the Queen's ban on profanity.

Pedro scarcely noticed him. With a muttered apology he hurried on, his eyes on a tall man walking slowly along the crowded street, head bent as if absorbed in thought.

"Captain Columbus!" Pedro called, a breathless little catch in his voice.

The man paused, turned, looked at him in momentary puzzlement, then with sudden recognition. A smile broke the gravity of his features.

"By San Fernando! My young friend from La Rábida!" He extended his hand and clasped Pedro's warmly. "I hardly recognized you in these surroundings, Pedro. I always associate you with the peaceful monastery."

Pedro beamed and made some response, he hardly knew what. Swiftly he scanned the well-remembered face—the gray-blue eyes, the aquiline nose, the strongly modeled, rather florid cheeks. The man was still as Pedro remembered him, save that his clothes were newer and smarter. His face, his air of quiet dignity, his resonant voice—these were unchanged. Even that "By San Fernando!" was familiar; the mild expletive had sprinkled his speech ever since Pedro had known him.

"I'm out for a stroll," Columbus said after a moment.

"Why not join me, Pedro, if you've nothing better to do?"

Pedro's heart turned a flip-flop. This was more than he'd dared hope for. He went warm all over as they moved off together.

Almost at once their talk turned to the Enterprise. Yes, Columbus assured him, everything was progressing satisfactorily. No, he expected no immediate decision, but the Queen had made her interest plain, and he was confident of the outcome. Of course, no action would be taken until the Queen's commission made its report. At this point a note of bitterness crept into his voice.

"Commissions! By San Fernando! I could have made a dozen voyages in the time I've spent arguing before commissions. And when at last they announce their verdict—what then? More delay! The Enterprise still must wait until Granada surrenders." He made a gesture of impatience. "As if the opening of the Indies were not more important than. . . ." His words trailed off to a brief frowning silence. But almost at once his manner brightened and he began speaking glowingly of his hopes.

Again, as so often in the old days at La Rábida, Pedro was caught up in the spell of the man's eloquence. Columbus could paint pictures with words—pictures of far places, of exotic cities, of Cathay and Cipango and the lands of spices and gold. Pedro listened entranced, and to his spellbound eyes the drab houses of Santa Fe were transformed into golden-domed palaces of the Orient. Those lands were not so far away, Columbus insisted—only a relatively short sail westward. Three small ships would be all he needed to make the voyage.

"Three ships!" he exclaimed. "Three small ships, and the crews to man them."

Pedro turned to him with his face alight. "You already have one of your crew, Captain Columbus."

"Eh? Who?" The tone was vague, inattentive.

"Why, me, of course."

There was no response. Pedro, suddenly uneasy, went on hesitantly. "Your promise, sir—it still holds, doesn't it?

"Promise? What promise?" The man seemed puzzled.

Pedro stared at him incredulously. "The promise you made to me, sir," he faltered. "You remember? You promised I could go with you on the voyage."

Columbus threw him a strange look. "Did I?" After a pause he said slowly, "Ah, so I did." Suddenly his tone grew soft. "Don't worry, lad. When I set sail for the Indies, rest assured you'll be with me." Then, as Pedro breathed deep in relief, the man added in so low a voice that the words were scarcely audible, "I'll always be in need of such faithfulness as yours."

There was a brief silence. When their talk resumed, Pedro sensed a subtle change in the other's attitude. Columbus had always been friendly, but now there was a companionable warmth in his manner he had never showed before. Pedro felt a new closeness between them. When they separated, nearly an hour later, Columbus's smile seemed almost wistful.

"We must see each other often, Pedro. Amid so much doubt and opposition, a friend's faith is something to value."

Pedro's emotions were confused as he made his way back to his quarters. He was happy at having had his long-anticipated talk with his idol. But a trace of dismay still lingered. How could Captain Columbus have forgotten his promise? How could something so all-important slip from anyone's mind? Hurt, puzzled, almost incredulous, Pedro groped for understanding.

And gradually it came.

That promise had been made carelessly, playfully, to a small boy. Columbus had forgotten it at once. Now, suddenly reminded of it, he realized that to Pedro the promise was a binding pledge, cherished through these past years. Perhaps for the first time he became aware that Pedro shared his dream, had made it his own. And his sudden new warmth of manner had expressed his grateful response.

Pedro's heart went soaring. The old promise had been renewed. Now, more strongly than ever, his own future was linked with that of Captain Columbus.

The sun was low in the west, almost ready to sink behind the hills. He watched its slow descent. Soon men would follow that sun westward, follow it to the farthermost horizon and beyond, to probe the secrets of the unknown sea. Captain Columbus would show the way. Captain Columbus —and Pedro Tegero.

The days passed uneventfully. Pedro spent much of the time with Paco and Chico, wandering about the city they had helped build—"To see what it looks like now that the dust has settled," Paco said. Their impressions of Santa Fe were less than enthusiastic.

"It seems so—so *stuffy*," was Pedro's verdict. "I miss those colored tents with all their bright pennons."

"So do I," Paco responded, and even the prosaic-minded Chico nodded agreement. The new city was drab, with no hint of the flamboyant pageantry of the camp it replaced. The only splashes of color were the standards of the commanders, fluttering over their respective quarters. Even the court precinct had a lackluster appearance.

"*Madre mia!*" Paco complained. "I don't even see any serving maids flouncing about."

But if Santa Fe was drab, it certainly wasn't solemn. During the first weeks following its completion, the atmosphere was almost festive. Music and song were heard more often than martial trumpets; games and contests took the place of arms drills. And the city looked more like a marketplace,than a military establishment, for merchants were arriving daily from the country's trade centers, their pack trains laden with wares. The merchants had something for every taste and purse, from jeweled swords and rich shawls to cheap trinkets and everyday necessities. Pedro and his comrades spent many an interested hour looking at the displays and making an occasional modest purchase.

But as time moved along, the days began to drag. The autumn rains began, with their spirit-dampening effect. Men wearied of inactivity, thought longingly of homes and families and the pursuits of peace.

October drew toward an end. There was plenty of time for idle talk now, especially when the rains kept the men indoors. Rumors, never at rest, began flying thick as moths around a lantern. The Moors had lost all hope—so said the rumors. Famine stalked Granada. Surrender was imminent, inevitable.

Pedro supposed the rumors were true, but wondered how in the world such details could reach Santa Fe. He took the question to Andrés, who as an old soldier might be expected to understand such matters. "How can we know what's going on in Granada, when it's sealed up like a bottle?" he demanded.

Andrés pursed his lips and considered for a moment. " 'The wind has a tongue,' " he quoted. Which, Pedro thought, was a neatly-applied adage, but didn't answer his question at all.

Pedro saw Columbus frequently. He had noticed that Columbus's strolls usually took him past the quarters of Gonzalo de Córdova and his cavalry company, not far from the central plaza. Pedro would station himself near the courtyard entrance, where he could watch the smartly-uniformed troopers and their horses, and sometimes don Gonzalo's superb white charger. Even if Captain Columbus didn't appear, Pedro felt that the time was well spent. There was no finer company in the army than Don Gonzalo's, and men often paused to look and admire when they passed the courtyard.

His talks with Columbus were usually brief, perhaps no more than an exchange of greetings, for the man often seemed pressed for time, or in a deep study which discouraged talk. But sometimes they would take a long and leisurely stroll, and the magic of their earlier meetings at La Rábida would be renewed. But now there was a difference, subtle but important. Columbus's attitude toward Pedro was no longer that of an adult to a child, but of one man to another.

The Queen's commission was still dragging on its deliberations. Its slowness worried Pedro. Columbus, however, though resentful of the delay, showed complete confidence in the outcome. So did Fray Juan, whom Pedro saw at intervals.

"Don't worry," the friar reassured the fretting youth. "At the moment the Enterprise is bogged down in a morass of argument, but it will launch out into clear waters when Granada surrenders."

When Granada surrenders! Everything must wait for that. Pedro felt a personal grievance against the stubborn Moors. They knew they hadn't a chance. Why didn't they give up now, and have done with it?

That sentiment was widespread among the troops of late. The abundant leisure, so welcome at first, began to seem too much of a good thing. Idleness was breeding boredom; rainy weather and cramped quarters made it worse. Nerves wore thin. Tempers shortened. Flare-ups were frequent, and despite the Queen's strict ban, hot words sometimes ended up in brawls.

"*Madre mia!*" Paco growled one afternoon, sweeping a sour glance around the crowded room. It was raining for the third straight day, and everyone who didn't have to be outdoors was huddled inside. "We're packed in here like crabs in a bucket. No wonder we're snapping at one another."

Pedro nodded, not bothering to speak. Chico gave an unperturbed yawn and curled up against the wall for a nap. Lack of space didn't worry Chico. He didn't need much space.

"*Madre mia!*" Paco repeated. "Another week of this and everybody'll be slitting everybody else's throat, just to pass the time."

Pedro responded with a mumble, barely audible, whereupon Paco, offended, moved off to seek more talkative company. For a moment or two Pedro felt properly contrite. Then he remembered that his spare shirt had a rent in the sleeve. Mending it would be as good a way as any to occupy the time. He rummaged in his gear for needle and thread and settled himself cross-legged on the floor. Just as he started to thread the needle, a soldier burst through the door with an excited shout. Pedro, startled, let the needle slip and nearly skewered his thumb. He smothered a yelp and muttered a word which he surely hadn't learned at the monastery. All eyes jerked toward the rain-soaked soldier.

"What a piece of news I've got!" The man paused for a moment, partly to catch a breath and partly for dramatic effect. "Who do you think just rode away from the city? Gonzalo de Córdova, that's who! Alone, mind you—and heading toward Granada!"

An instant stir of interest swept the room. "You're sure it was don Gonzalo?" someone asked.

"I'm not blind, am I?" The soldier wrenched off his streaming jerkin with a vigor that sent the spray flying, spattering the comrades who had crowded close. "I was standing sentry duty on the battlements, and saw him ride out toward Granada. And that isn't all! At almost the same instant a horseman rode out *from* Granada—where no one has stirred outside the walls for months. As soon as they sighted each other they angled off in a direction that would bring them together in the hills. It was plain enough—they had a meeting arranged."

A babble of excitement burst out. No one was bored now. Pedro stopped sucking his punctured thumb and listened eagerly to the comments flying back and forth.

"There's only one reason don Gonzalo would be meeting with a Moor—to discuss surrender terms."

"To be sure. Don Gonzalo is the logical man for that. He speaks Arabic like a born Moslem."

"And the Moors trust him. He and Boabdil are friends."

Pedro's heart began beating faster as the significance of the words sank in. Of course! Don Gonzalo's mission could mean only one thing—the enemy was ready to talk terms. Then a puzzled thought struck him. He turned to Andrés, who was sitting nearby, an unwonted trace of animation in his melancholy face.

"How do you suppose the meeting was arranged, with Granada closed up tight?" Pedro asked him.

Andrés blinked his sad eyes, then repeated his usual proverb. " 'The wind has a tongue.' "

It was an apt response, Pedro thought, but not very enlightening. He turned his attention back to the clamor around him. The men had seized eagerly on the incident, giving it a meaning to fit their own wishes, almost convincing themselves that it guaranteed an immediate end to the war. Pedro was as eager as anyone to be convinced. If don Gonzalo's mission meant an end to the war, it also meant. . . .

His ears grew deaf to the talk. The crowded room faded from his sight. His vivid imagination was carrying him across a trackless sea and landing him on the enchanted shores of the Indies.

He sat there for a long time, needle in limp fingers, the shirt draped unnoticed across his legs. Gradually it dawned on him that the room had grown lighter. It was less crowded, too—nearly empty, in fact. Chico was still snoozing, but everybody else was seeking the open air, for the rain had subsided to a barely noticeable sprinkle. Their voices carried through the open door, still discussing don Gonzalo's mission.

Suddenly it occurred to Pedro that Captain Columbus would know something definite about the matter, close as he was to court circles. This was the time of day he might be encountered. Pedro put the shirt away, its ripped sleeve still gaping, and hurried outside. The sky was still soggy-looking and dripping slightly, but Pedro didn't notice. He headed briskly in the direction of the court precinct.

The rain had stopped completely when he took his usual station near Gonzalo de Córdova's quarters. The street there was more crowded than usual, and the snatches of talk he overheard all concerned don Gonzalo's rendezvous with the Moor. Already the incident was common knowledge. Men went out of their way to pass close to the courtyard entrance and scan the row of stalls at the rear, assuring themselves that don Gonzalo's horse was indeed absent.

Pedro walked slowly back and forth, looking often toward the central plaza. But the tall figure he was looking for was nowhere to be seen. The sun, visible as a brighter splotch in the overhead haze, dropped slowly toward the misted hori-

zon. He had almost decided that the wait had been wasted
when he saw Columbus some distance away, coming toward
the plaza. His thrill of pleasure was at once subdued. Evidently Captain Columbus had already finished his stroll and
was now returning to his quarters. There would be no time
for the leisurely chat Pedro had hoped for.

Pedro hurried to meet him. Columbus greeted him
warmly, but showed no intention of lingering, so Pedro
wasted no preliminaries before questioning him about don
Gonzalo. To his delight, Columbus confirmed the speculations of the troops.

"Yes, Pedro, it's true—don Gonzalo is meeting with an
emissary from Granada." The keen eyes gleamed with suppressed excitement. "The meeting is an open secret among
those close to the court."

"You mean they're holding a peace talk right this minute?"

"Perhaps it is premature to call it a 'peace talk,' but it is
undoubtedly a step in that direction. It is said that don
Gonzalo will be entrusted with all the necessary negotiations.
A delicate task, to be sure. Probably it will drag on for some
time." His tone took on an edge of bitterness. "Such matters
usually do—and who should know better than I!"

"But at least the talks are started," Pedro pointed out
eagerly.

"Yes. And that means the war's end is in sight. Boabdil
would never consent to talk terms if he didn't intend to
surrender."

Pedro's heart soared. Then he looked faintly worried.

"Now if only the Queen's commission gives a favorable report!"

"I have no fear about that. And the Queen's personal approval is assured, once Granada surrenders."

"Then the way will soon be cleared for the Enterprise!"

"Yes. Soon!" Excitement flared higher in the man's face. "As soon as my terms are met!"

Perhaps in the surge of excitement the words slipped out involuntarily, for the instant they were spoken his lips tightened and his manner turned grim.

Pedro threw him a startled glance, not certain he had heard aright. "Your—your terms, sir?" he faltered.

"My terms." The tone was defiant. Columbus plunged on hurriedly, as if, having said so much, he was unable to stop. "And my terms will not be mild. Once I would have been satisfied with a modest reward. But that was before I wasted six years of my life begging for support. I will beg no longer—now I will demand. And if my demands are not met. . . ." He shrugged disdainfully. "There are other countries than Spain which I can serve."

Pedro was shocked into speechlessness. A long moment passed before he managed a hesitant question. "What—what terms will you ask, sir?"

A guarded note crept into the man's voice. "It is not yet time to outline my terms, Pedro. But this I will say—I will demand my rightful share of all the wealth and honor and power that the Enterprise shall win for Spain. Not only for myself, but for my descendants."

There was a short silence. Suddenly Columbus seemed to

notice Pedro's stricken look. Shedding his grim manner, he
smiled reassuringly. "Don't worry, Pedro. The Enterprise is
in no danger. My demands will be met—I am confident of
it."

Pedro forced a semblance of a smile. "Y-yes, sir. Of
course." Mechanically he responded to the other's good-by
and stumbled away, his mind a whirl of bewilderment. Columbus had misread the motive for his dismay. It wasn't
concern for the Enterprise—not entirely. It was mainly the
shock of disillusionment.

So his idol's splendid dream was for sale—something to be
bargained for, auctioned off to the highest bidder! So it
wasn't the lure of the great unknown which drew Columbus
on, but the lure of wealth and self-aggrandizement! The
thoughts raced through his mind against his will, refusing to
be checked. Pedro fought them, hated them, but couldn't
subdue them.

Had the man's detractors been right, after all? Was he
merely an ambitious schemer, eager to risk a reckless venture
for the sake of the spoils? No, no, no! That Pedro could not
accept—or would not. But what else was he to think, after
what he'd just heard?

Of course, he told himself desperately, he might have
construed the man's remarks unfairly. After all, one couldn't
find fault with Captain Columbus for demanding a just
recompense. But that argument fell apart even as he raised it.
There would be no need to demand a just recompense—that
would be granted as a matter of course. The Sovereigns
weren't niggardly toward those who served them. No, Captain Columbus had made it plain that he would carry out the

Enterprise only on his own terms. And those terms—he'd said it in so many words—would not be mild.

Pedro tried to close his mind to the thoughts. They were unworthy, treacherous, he rebuked himself. Somehow he still believed in his idol. But the troubled doubts surged steadily against his faith like waves surging against a rock.

Renewed Faith

"That's a smart-looking belt, the one with the worked leather," Pedro observed.

"I'd rather have the one with the fancy buckle," Chico said, after a pause for comparison.

Paco assumed a self-righteous expression. "You two are both alike—only interested in what you can use yourselves. Me, I'm looking for gifts to make other people happy— especially if they're young and pretty."

The three were wandering among the merchants' displays, trying to decide what they would buy if they had the money. Having passed judgment on the belts, Pedro and Chico turned their attention to some poniards with carved handles. Paco's interest was divided between two exquisite silk scarves, one the color of a summer sky—"for Dolores, to match her eyes," he explained—and the other as red as an Andalusian cherry—"for Carmen, to match her lips." Pedro suspected that both fair damsels were as nonexistent as Paco's funds.

After a pleasant and inexpensive hour, the three left the displays and moved to where a barber had set up shop at the edge of the street. Besides the waiting customers, a number of loiterers were gathered about, for barbers dispensed news, gossip, and rumors, usually with a fine disregard as to which was which. The trio paused with one accord to listen and learn. They quickly caught the drift of the conversation.

"I hear that Moorish officials are meeting with don Gonzalo more and more often," someone said.

"You hear correctly." The barber's air of authority implied that he was fully informed on the matter. "Don Gonzalo is in and out of Santa Fe several times a week, and riders are constantly seen leaving Granada. Boabdil's emissaries, of course. They have a meeting place arranged somewhere in the hills. The exact location is a deep dark secret, naturally, but it's no secret what's going on there."

"One would think the whole thing would be threshed out and settled by this time," someone else observed.

"Oh, there is much to be discussed." The barber poised his razor over his customer's cheek and nodded sagely. "These matters can't be settled overnight, you know. However, I'm told by those who know that the talks are progressing quite well."

One of the loiterers cocked a skeptical eyebrow. "How can anyone know how the talks are progressing—or even if talks are being held?"

The razor stroked the customer's cheek, clearing a swath through suds and stubble. The barber winked knowingly. " 'The wind has a tongue,' " he said.

Pedro felt a mild exasperation. That talkative wind again!

"*Vaya!*" he exclaimed as the three friends moved on. "Everybody claims to know everything that's going on, but nobody has the faintest idea where the information comes from."

Paco chuckled. "It's a good system. If you can't answer a

question, never admit it. Just come up with a pithy proverb, and people will never suspect that you're just as ignorant as they are."

Chico squinted at the sun. "It's nearly suppertime. Let's get back to quarters."

Pedro nodded, then suddenly changed his mind. "I think I'll wait awhile. I'll be along later."

Paco gave a disdainful little sniff. "Captain Columbus, of course." It was a name that still rankled Paco.

"Naturally, it's Captain Columbus," Pedro said good-naturedly. "In case I'm late, save me a share of supper, will you?" Paco answered with a grunt, Chico with an amiable nod, and Pedro divided a grin between them as he turned into a side street that would lead to a main thoroughfare.

Now that he was alone, his mood grew thoughtful. He'd decided on impulse to look for Captain Columbus, but suddenly he wasn't sure he really wanted to meet him. For it seemed of late that their every meeting raised fresh misgivings. Columbus, once having dropped his guard, was less reticent now about the rewards he anticipated from the Enterprise. He spoke of them often, not in bald statements, but in veiled remarks which were just as revealing. Personal gain meant more to him than the Enterprise itself, Pedro thought, and then hated himself for thinking it.

Troubled, he walked slowly toward the broad thoroughfare which led to the court precinct. At first he barely noticed the distance-muffled clatter of hoofs coming from the direction of the east gate. Then a faint surprise stirred. That was the gate which faced Granada. Why would riders be entering the city from that direction? The hoofbeats became loud and sharp, and an instant later two horsemen galloped past the intersection ahead. Pedro recognized one of them at once, for Gonzalo de Córdova on his white charger was unmistakeable even in a passing glimpse.

Pedro hurried to the intersection, swung around the corner, and gazed after the riders, stretching his neck to see past the intervening figures. The mounted pair passed don Gonzalo's quarters and rode on into the central plaza. They drew rein, leaped from their saddles just outside the Sovereigns' quarters, and disappeared through the doorway before a startled attendant gathered enough wits to grasp the horses' bridles.

All along the thoroughfare, men had stopped to stare as the two clattered past. Now the street stirred into activity again, humming with excited talk. The riders' haste made it plain that their business was extremely important. Don Gonzalo had of course been conferring with Boabdil's emissary. Perhaps final terms had been agreed upon. Perhaps. . . .

Pedro had forgotten his purpose in coming here. He walked on rapidly toward the plaza, his attention fixed on the Sovereigns' quarters, trying to guess what was going on inside. Suddenly a familiar voice sounded just a pace or two ahead.

"Wake up, Pedro, before you collide with someone!"

Pedro came to himself with a start. "Fray Juan!" He grinned, somewhat sheepishly. "I'm sorry, Fray Juan—I didn't notice you. You see, don Gonzalo just rode past and—"

"*Rode* past? *Flew* past, I would say!" Fray Juan flicked a glance toward the court precinct, then turned back to Pedro. There was a glint of excitement in his eyes.

"I rather thought I'd find you here, Pedro. You're looking for Captain Columbus, of course. But you're not likely to find him this evening. Just now Captain Columbus is a very busy man—and, I might add, a very happy one." Fray Juan beamed. "The Queen's commission has reported at last, and favorably!"

Pedro didn't answer. He couldn't. His heart had soared into his throat. But his shining face said more than any words he could have spoken.

"The report was delivered this morning," Fray Juan went on. "The commission has decided that the project is feasible, and recommends that it be approved by the Royal Council."

Pedro found his voice. "Then everything's all settled!"

Fray Juan's eyes twinkled. "Not so fast, Pedro. Remember, the final decision will be up to Their Highnesses. And don Ferdinand is still quite lukewarm to the whole idea."

"But doña Isabella isn't!"

"No. Doña Isabella isn't—and on that fact we can safely pin our hopes."

They started walking slowly back and forth, staying just outside the plaza, as if reluctant to go farther from the center of developments. Fray Juan's face was thoughtful.

"Even so, Pedro, it's a bit premature to say that everything is settled. I'm afraid there may still be obstacles ahead."

"Obstacles?" Pedro's high spirits subsided somewhat. "But the commission has approved. And the war is practically over. What possible obstacle could there be now?"

"Perhaps the greatest obstacle of all," came the slow reply. "Perhaps Captain Columbus's own pride."

Pedro was dumfounded. He looked at the friar in puzzled protest. Fray Juan raised his hand in a gesture of reassurance.

"Mind you, Pedro—I don't fear for the final outcome. But Captain Columbus hints that he intends to make certain demands—and that they will not be modest. That will doubtless cause an unforeseen delay. However, I'm certain that the Queen will accede to any reasonable demands."

Pedro's eyes searched the monk's face. "And what if the demands aren't reasonable?" he asked quietly.

There was a brief hesitation, but Fray Juan replied with firm confidence. "Even in that case, I am sure the Queen will accede." He went on reflectively. "I know Captain Columbus. He can be stubborn. Whatever conditions he makes, he'll give up the Enterprise rather than lessen them by one iota. But I know doña Isabella, too. She does not readily give up her hopes—and her hopes for the Enterprise are high. Another thing—Columbus has powerful friends at court, who have great influence with the Queen." Fray Juan's manner lightened and the smile returned to his face. Just as I say, Pedro, there may still be obstacles. But obstacles can be overcome."

Pedro's confidence came flooding back, but the elation of a few moments ago was gone. The sense of disillusionment which had nagged him of late surged up with new intensity. What Fray Juan had just said confirmed the misgivings he had tried vainly to suppress. His face sobered, his voice became low and troubled.

"I'd have thought Captain Columbus would be the last person on earth to put anything in the way of the Enterprise. I never expected *him* to be so . . . so. . . ." He left the sentence hanging.

Fray Juan looked at him keenly. "You're disappointed in Captain Columbus, aren't you, Pedro?"

Pedro nodded unhappily. "He seems so changed, Fray Juan. Back at La Rábida he was always talking about the Indies, and exploring the Unknown Sea, and bringing the Faith to pagan lands. He still talks of those things, of course. But now. . . ." Again his words trailed off.

"But now he also talks of wealth and honors—is that it?"

Pedro didn't answer directly. "He—he has changed."

Fray Juan looked at him without speaking for a moment, then shook his head slowly. "No, Pedro. Captain Columbus has not changed. It is you who have changed." He smiled at the questioning surprise in Pedro's face. "At La Rábida you were a child. In your eyes Columbus was a paragon, whose every word spoke of lofty purpose. But now the child has become a man. Your experience is broader, your perception keener. You began to see your paragon in a truer light—his lofty stature cut down to life-size. And you are disappointed because he no longer seems the Columbus you imagined him to be. Pedro, Pedro—such a Columbus has never existed, except in your imagination."

Pedro listened in silence, striving for understanding. Fray Juan's smile rested on him briefly, then it faded to grave earnestness. "Keep your faith in him, Pedro—he has detractors enough. Some have distrusted him. Some have mocked

him. Some have even cast doubt on his mental soundness."
A shadow of anger crossed his face. "There are those who call
him an ambitious adventurer—and they are right! He *is* an
ambitious adventurer, and thank God for it. A man without
ambition is a clod. A man who shrinks from adventure is a
coward."

A regretful note crept into Fray Juan's voice. "It is true,
perhaps, that Columbus is overly concerned with his own
aggrandizement. I could wish that he had a truer sense of
values. But I could make that same wish for myself—for
you—for all men. None of us is free from faults, Pedro.
Don't expect Columbus to be."

Pedro drew a long breath. "Maybe I did expect too much
of him," he said slowly. "It's just that—well, I always
thought of him as such a great man, who would do such
great things."

"If he is a great man, it is not because of what he may or
may not do. He may achieve everything, or he may achieve
nothing. But he is a man with a dream, Pedro—and with the
courage to fight for that dream. The battle may be lost, but
he has waged it with all his strength. The dream may be a
delusion, but he has followed it with faith. It is there that his
greatness lies."

Fray Juan paused, and for a few moments neither spoke.
Then the friar looked at Pedro with kindly seriousness. "You
understand what I'm trying to say, don't you, Pedro?"

"I'm beginning to," Pedro answered. The nagging doubts
were gone, and he knew they would never assail him again.

They talked a little longer, sometimes lapsing into companionable silence. Sunset was painting the sky over the

city's western wall when presently they said good night. Fray
Juan's parting smile was benign. Pedro's was grateful and
untroubled.

Pedro started toward his quarters, walking slowly, thoughtfully. Then on a sudden impulse he moved to the edge of the
street and sat down on a shadowed doorstep. He felt a need
for solitude. Darkness was closing in, the early darkness that
hinted of approaching winter. Lamps and candles began to
flicker through windows, and the lanterns hung over gateways
were being lighted. The street was nearly deserted now, but
from the walled courtyards between the houses came the
sounds of voices and activity. It was suppertime, and Pedro
was getting hungry, but still he lingered where he was.
Supper could wait. Right now he wanted to think.

His talk with Fray Juan had made him understand many
things, about himself as well as about Captain Columbus.
He had indeed set an impossibly high standard for Columbus. In his childish hero-worship he'd been blinded to reality,
dazzled by the splendor of the man's dream. Captain Columbus wasn't a demigod to be idolized, but a man to be
admired, with a man's faults and a man's virtues.

And—Pedro realized it with something of surprise—he
really liked Captain Columbus better that way.

Staring into the deepening darkness, he became gradually
oblivious of his surroundings. Instead, he saw a vast ocean
and a far-off horizon. He saw three small ships on that ocean,
challenging its mystery, sailing toward that beckoning west
which was also east. And he, Pedro Tegero, was on one of
those ships! He, Pedro Tegero, had a part in the greatest
adventure men had ever dared!

It was an overwhelming thought. Pedro was caught up in its wonder, lost to all sense of time and place. Then, like a mist diffused by wind, the spell was rifted by the click of hoofbeats on cobblestones. He looked up reluctantly, wanting to cling to his reverie. Don Gonzalo and his companion had left the royal quarters and were riding slowly out of the plaza. At once Pedro came alert, his mind filled with eager speculation. What news had they brought the Sovereigns? Good or bad, it must have been important.

He watched the pair approach, two dark shadows, faintly lighted at intervals as they rode past the scattered lanterns. Their features were indistinguishable, but even in the darkness don Gonzalo on his splendid mount made a striking picture, his companion quite undistinguished by comparison. Pedro leaned forward to watch them as they passed.

But evidently they weren't going to pass. They were guiding their mounts toward the edge of the street, straight in Pedro's direction. All at once he realized that it was don Gonzalo's doorstep he was sitting on. He sprang up hastily, then immediately wished he hadn't, for the movement brought him out of the concealing shadow and into the light of the lanterns that flanked the courtyard entrance. The horses shied slightly at his sudden appearance, and he heard a surprised exclamation from one of the riders. He started away, angry at having shown himself. If he'd remained quiet, they'd have ridden into the courtyard without even noticing him.

He heard a brief murmured exchange between the two, then again the clack-clack of hoofs. But only one set of hoofbeats turned into the courtyard—the other clattered up alongside Pedro. So, he thought resentfully, they must make a big to-do over nothing! He stopped and looked up defiantly, braced for a reprimand. Instead, a delighted voice sang out.

"Pedro! It *is* you! For a moment I wasn't sure."

Pedro stared in bewilderment as the rider swung down from the saddle. Surely he knew that voice! The lantern glow, which Pedro was facing, struck the other from behind, leaving his face shadowed save for a sidelighted cheek—high-boned, smooth-shaven, crinkled by a vast smile. Yet, shadowed though it was, the face was familiar.

Pedro gasped, then gave a glad cry of recognition.

"*Felipe!*"

Explanations

Five full minutes had passed, but Pedro was still bewildered. Felipe led the way into the lantern-lit courtyard and turned his mount over to a groom. He indicated a bench by a row of stalls, a little apart from the bustle and babble of the troopers, and the two sat down and beamed at each other, the lantern glow bright on their faces.

"*Caray*—your beard's gone!" Pedro exclaimed. "No wonder I didn't recognize you—especially in the dark."

Felipe chuckled and fingered his hairless chin. "Beards are for Moors, not for a self-respecting Spaniard. I shaved mine off—it had served its purpose." His eyes twinkled as they met Pedro's puzzled gaze. "All right, Pedro. Just make yourself comfortable and I'll tell you the whole story."

"I'm comfortable, and I'm listening," Pedro told him.

Felipe's smile broadened briefly, then his face took on a faraway look. There was a short silence. Pedro waited. After a moment Felipe began his story.

"As you know, Pedro, when I escaped from Granada I intended to reach the camp and join the Spanish army. Well, as you also know, I reached the camp—with a punctured arm. There I was, disabled, without resources, facing a future that looked anything but bright. And besides all that, it

seemed I was regarded with suspicion in certain quarters."
He flicked a teasing glance at Pedro. "I rather think those
quarters included *you, amigo*."

Pedro grinned, a little sheepishly, and made no denial.

Felipe's manner sobered. "I've come to be grateful for that
suspicion—it brought me into contact with don Gonzalo."
His tone warmed as he spoke the name. "I liked don Gonzalo the first time I saw him, while I was still in that hospital
cot. He told me frankly that he'd come to check into my
story. I was surprised to learn that I'd stirred interest in such
high quarters—for it was plain that don Gonzalo was something of a personage. However, I told him the facts, and after
he'd asked a few searching questions he seemed satisfied.
Allah y' fazak, he's a man who knows the truth when he
hears it."

Pedro's lips quirked. Felipe's speech was still sprinkled
with Arabic. Felipe, not noticing, went on.

"Don Gonzalo dropped the subject of my personal history
and started questioning me about the situation in Granada. I
told him what I knew, and what I guessed. I could see that
he was studying me all the while. Presently he said something that puzzled me. 'You're observant—that helps.' Suddenly he leaned forward and lowered his voice, so that only I
could hear him. 'You say you had intended to join the army.
Since your wound makes that impossible, are you willing to
serve our cause in another way?'

" 'Willing and eager,' I told him, wondering what in the
world he was leading up to.

"He looked me straight in the eyes. 'I warn you, it won't
be safe or easy. If that scares you, forget the whole thing. But

if you can stand up to a bit of danger and hardship without cringing, then come to see me just as soon as you're able.' Then he studied my face for a minute and added, 'Meanwhile, it would be well if you would start letting your beard grow.' "

Pedro's eyebrows shot up. So there had been a reason for Felipe's refusal to get rid of that beard!

Felipe plucked at his cheek absently, the way he used to pluck at his beard. "That left me more puzzled than ever, but when I tried to question him he only smiled and said he'd explain later. When he got up to leave he gave me an emphatic order. 'Nothing I have said is to be repeated to anyone. That's important. You'll be of no use to me if you're unable to keep a secret.' "

Felipe paused, his eyes twinkling. "Well, I was able to keep a secret—as you yourself should know, Pedro. You tried more than once to pry something out of me, but I wasn't very talkative, eh?"

"About as talkative as a shellfish. But go on, Felipe—I'm curious."

"*Bismillah!* So was I. I reported to don Gonzalo just as soon as I was able to make it to his tent, and we had frequent talks from then on, but it was some time before I learned anything definite. I understood why, of course—don Gonzalo was sizing me up carefully before trusting me with any information. I'm happy to say that I passed the test, and finally he told me what he had in mind.

"I learned that don Gonzalo had a heavy responsibility on his shoulders. Because he knew the Moors so well, the Sovereigns relied on him to get information about the situation

in Granada. Was there enough food to withstand a long
siege? Was the city making ready for active resistance? Was
morale holding firm? Above all, was there any chance of an
early surrender? Many such questions must be answered
somehow.

"Don Gonzalo explained that he faced a problem. 'I can
get information of a sort from enemy captives, or Moorish
renegades who switch sides for personal gain, but it goes
without saying that their reports can't be trusted. I must be
certain that my information is reliable. And the only way to
be certain is to have my own observer in Granada—a man I
can trust implicitly. For some time I have been seeking
quietly but desperately for just such a man. I think, Felipe
Luza, that I have found him.' "

Felipe paused briefly, soberly. "Well, Pedro, by that time I
saw what was coming, and I don't mind admitting I didn't
like it. Don Gonzalo started ticking off my qualifications on
his fingers. 'You speak Arabic fluently. You are thoroughly
familiar with Granada and with Moorish customs. You are
observant, as I've learned by my questions. You are resourceful, else you wouldn't have escaped. And with that dark skin
and black beard you could readily pass as a Moor if you dress
the part. That leaves one all-important question. Will you
undertake the mission?' "

Felipe drew a long breath. "I did some hard, fast thinking.
Granada was the last place in the world I wanted to set foot
in—especially as a spy. If I were recognized, I'd be a slave
again. And if my mission should be discovered, they'd hang
me higher than the Alhambra.

"Don Gonzalo was watching me, as if he knew exactly

what was passing through my mind. 'Don't decide hastily,' he said. 'Consider the risks well.'

"Believe me, I was doing just that. But there are some things a man can't shirk. I told him I wasn't afraid of the risks." With a flash of dry humor, Felipe added, "That was the only time I've ever lied to don Gonzalo."

He was serious again at once. "Don Gonzalo got down to details then. I was to go to Granada and lose myself among the people, become a Moor among Moors. I was to keep my eyes and ears open for whatever might develop—keep a finger on the city's pulsebeat, so to speak. Above all else, I was to watch for any sign of readiness to surrender. This last point was the most important to don Gonzalo. 'Frankly, I'm puzzled,' he told me. 'I expected some peace feeler from the Moors before now. They face starvation and death, with no chance of winning. Yet they seem determined to hold out to the bitter end. There must be a reason, and for the present your major concern will be to learn what it is.' I was to start the assignment as soon as I was in fit enough condition. Meanwhile, we'd use the time to work out the many, many details."

Pedro remembered how often he had visited the hospital and found Felipe absent. It was plain now—Felipe hadn't been exploring the camp, as he'd claimed.

Felipe went on. "As it turned out, my departure was hastened a bit by the King's sudden decision to destroy the parkland outside Granada. When I heard about that, I realized that it would give me an ideal opportunity to slip into the city under cover of the confusion. You were with me at the time—remember?"

"I remember," Pedro said with a faint smile. Many things were falling into place.

"My departure was scheduled for the following week," Felipe explained. "But I hurried to don Gonzalo at once and suggested that we advance our plans a bit. He agreed, and we acted fast. Luckily, most of our preparations had already been made. Don Gonzalo had Moorish clothes ready for me, and some other necessities, but there were many last-minute details to be worked out, and our time was short. I didn't return to the hospital at all, but stayed with don Gonzalo, shaping up final arrangements."

Pedro felt a stab of self-reproach. He'd been so sure that Felipe had used that period to warn the Moors of the impending ravages. The thought prompted another. "How do you suppose the Moors learned what we were planning, Felipe? They were waiting in ambush when we got to the park."

"A spy must have warned them. Doubtless they had agents planted in our camp to keep an eye on us, just as I was planning to keep an eye on them. Spying works both ways, you know." He cocked an expressive eyebrow, then continued his story.

"Things worked out as planned. I left the camp on the far side from Granada—with all the coming and going there, I wasn't noticed. Then I circled around at a distance and headed for Granada. On the way I shed my Spanish clothes and stowed them where I could retrieve them on my way back—if I should be lucky enough to come back. I slipped into the city after dark, and before daybreak was sleeping in an alley, as Moorish-looking in my turban and burnous as Boabdil himself—though considerably more ragged."

Pedro was puzzled. "How did you get into the city, with all the gates closed?"

"Through one of the culverts in the wall. The stream was all but dry at that season. That has always been a favored passage for people who want to avoid the guards at the gates."

Pedro nodded, remembering Hernán del Pulgar's furtive entry into Granada to hang a placard on the door of a mosque.

Felipe continued. "At first I was constantly uneasy, afraid of being recognized. But a beard and a dirty face and ragged clothes made a good disguise, and a close-drawn burnous-hood helped. The city was swarming with refugees, so it was a simple matter to pass as one of them. Of course, I stayed away from the neighborhood where I'd lived before, though even there I'd probably have been safe, for the whole city was in a state of shock and confusion after that battle in the parkland."

Felipe touched only briefly on how he had haunted public gathering places, watching and listening, slowly gleaning the information he had been sent for. Pedro could guess much that Felipe only hinted at, of hardship and danger, of living the derelict existence of a refugee, sleeping in doorways and streets, barely subsisting on the scanty rations doled out from the government storehouses. Felipe told how the fire in the Spanish camp had raised hope among the Moors that the siege would be lifted, and how hope had ebbed when a permanent city began rising from the ashes. Yet even then, despite the grief and sickness and hunger that reigned in

Granada, the people refused to admit the possibility of defeat. This blind conviction had baffled Felipe at first. But before long he had learned its cause.

"It was a *santón*—a 'holy man,' " he explained. "He had appeared from nowhere, claiming that Allah had revealed to him that Granada would triumph. Crowds would gather and listen spellbound to his ranting. He looked like something out of a nightmare—shaggy, wild-eyed, wearing nothing but a verminous sheep hide and a thick coating of dirt. He was half crazed, of course, but that only added to his prestige—to the Moors, madness is a sign of heaven's special favor. He leaped and danced and waved his skinny arms, shouting that Allah had spoken to him and promised a miracle—that Granada need only wait, and soon the Spanish infidels would be crushed."

Pedro's eyes widened. "And they believed him? *Caray*—they must have been as mad as he!"

"Oh, Moors often put blind faith in oracles. He had little influence on the more sophisticated classes, but to the common people, that *santón's* prediction made Granada's victory certain as sunrise. And, of course, it dashed any hope for an early surrender. As soon as I was sure of the situation, I slipped out of the city and brought the discouraging news to don Gonzalo. It hit him hard, I think more for the Moors' sake than for our own. As he put it, 'We can afford to wait. They can't.'

"As you know, Pedro, don Gonzalo has many friends among the Moors, including Boabdil himself. Because of this, he explained, the Sovereigns had proposed that he try to get peace talks started. But the news I had brought made it plain that nothing could be done as matters stood. Don Gonzalo was convinced that Boabdil was ready to talk terms, simply to spare his people further suffering. But, the people's mood being what it was, Boabdil's hands were tied. It was tragic. Thousands would suffer, many would die, because of a madman's ravings." Felipe shook his head soberly.

"I rested a day or two," he continued, "then went back to Granada. The weeks passed, and hunger and disease got worse, yet the people clung to their trust in that 'holy man.' He raved on, still claiming that he was the voice of Allah, promising that Granada would be saved.

"I was always alert for anything unusual, otherwise I wouldn't have noticed the handful of men who appeared one day while the *santón* was haranguing the people. They stayed at the edge of the crowd, watching and listening, and it was plain that they didn't like what they saw and heard. It struck me that they looked surprisingly well-fed, considering that everybody else was so hungry-looking. They were dressed simply, but I'd have staked my next meal that they were nobles. They were back again at intervals for a week or so, always keeping to the edge of the crowd, watching closely but avoiding notice. Something was afoot, that was certain —and I had a fair suspicion what it was."

Pedro leaned forward in eager curiosity. Felipe was staring off into space, as if he saw again the scenes he was describing.

"And then one night the *santón* disappeared. He has never been seen since." Felipe's voice was somber. "There were bloodstains in the doorway where he'd been sleeping. What had happened was plain enough. Certain Moors in high

places were convinced that the swiftest way to peace was to
dispose of that *santón*. Perhaps it was the only way to save
the people from their own delusions. But there was something pathetic in their reaction. They were stunned at first,
then crushed. Their courage died with the poor crazed fa-
natic who had inspired it. But, *Allah y' fazak*, now at last
they had to face the truth—Granada's only salvation lay in
surrender.

"I lost no time bringing don Gonzalo the news. He was
jubilant. It confirmed his conviction that the Moorish leaders
were ready to talk terms. Now, he said, it was time for the
next phase of our operations. He wanted to get negotiations
started without delay. As an opening move, he would write
to Boabdil at once." Felipe paused. The lantern light showed
a wry little smile on his lips. "I'd been sitting there nodding
agreement to everything he said, but now I suddenly stopped
nodding. Don Gonzalo was explaining, very casually, that I
was to deliver the letter!

"*Bismillah!* All I could do was stare at him with my mouth
open. He assured me that this assignment would be far less
dangerous than the first, since I would no longer be acting as
a spy, but as an emissary. Which, I thought, was nicely
put—but would the Moors perceive the distinction? Don
Gonzalo also assured me that, being his emissary, I should
have no difficulty in reaching Boabdil. He added that Boabdil
would give me complete protection. Reassuring words, Pedro
—but somehow I wasn't at all reassured.

"However, it turned out to be surprisingly easy. I slipped
into the city by night and was at the Alhambra gates the next
morning. The situation called for boldness, so I decided to be

bold. I showed the guards my letter and explained that it was for none other than Boabdil. Naturally they were suspicious, but it was a very important-looking letter, with a very important-looking seal, so after searching me and finding no concealed weapons, they started passing me and the letter from one official to another, each a little higher in rank." Felipe chuckled. "It was like going up a ladder.

"And so, by degrees, I finally reached Boabdil. Pedro! The luxury of that Moorish court! But amid it all, every face looked grim and hopeless. Boabdil made a striking impression on me. He seemed proud, yet pathetic, and his dignified manner couldn't hide the strain he was under. Just as don Gonzalo had said, he treated me with every courtesy. I lived in the Alhambra for several days, waiting for his reply to don Gonzalo's letter. The Alhambra was a familiar sight to me from the outside. But *inside. . . !* Courts and fountains and— Oh, I wouldn't even attempt to describe it.

"Anyway, Boabdil sent for me a few days later and gave me a letter to deliver to don Gonzalo. He furnished me with a horse, and a party of men-at-arms escorted me past the gate, so my departure from Granada was considerably more dignified than my entry. In my eagerness, I nearly came dashing back to Santa Fe in burnous and turban, but luckily I remembered to stop at my cache and change back to my Spanish clothes. Then I made for don Gonzalo's quarters as fast as my mount would carry me—and a few days later, peace talks got started."

Felipe drew a long breath. "That's about all, Pedro. The talks were held in an abandoned hamlet in the hills. Don Gonzalo took over one of the houses, with a few trusted retainers. He had me stay there too, so I could sit in on the discussions. Someone had to keep a record of the proceedings, and since I'm familiar with both languages, and write a fair hand, the choice fell on me."

Pedro clapped his hand to his forehead in an exaggerated gesture of astonishment. "*Madre mia!* You've really become a man of consequence."

Felipe grinned and let the remark pass. "I stayed at the meeting place, but don Gonzalo had to go back and forth constantly, first conferring with the Sovereigns, then with Boabdil's emissaries. He had a knotty task, hammering out terms that would be acceptable to both sides. Everything had to be kept secret, of course, but with don Gonzalo continually riding in and out of Santa Fe, rumors were bound to start flying. 'The wind has a tongue,' you know."

Pedro's lips twitched. "Yes. So I've heard." Then he dropped his frivolous manner. "But seriously, Felipe, you can be proud of what you've done. Don Gonzalo must surely be grateful—and Their Highnesses, too."

"They have assured me that they are. But to my mind, it's I who should be grateful to don Gonzalo, for giving me the chance." A sudden lilt sounded in his voice. "Don Gonzalo has asked me to stay in his service, Pedro."

"Wonderful!" Pedro exclaimed. "Why, don Gonzalo's men are the pride of the army."

"That they are. I was amazed when he proposed it. I told him I'd like nothing better, if he could use a man with a bad arm. He only laughed at that. He said, 'I've got scores of fighting men, but you're the only man I can rely on as a spy, as an emissary, and as a secretary.'" Felipe's smile flashed out again, then was gone. The dim light showed a pensive expression on his face. "Things looked bleak to me a few months ago. I was partially disabled, owned nothing, had no home or family. I didn't like to think of what might lie ahead. But how everything is changed! Don Gonzalo offers me a future brighter than I could ever have hoped for."

"You've earned it," Pedro said fervently.

Felipe shrugged off that statement. "There's no one I'd rather serve than don Gonzalo. He's a great captain, Pedro."

"Yes," Pedro agreed. "A great captain."

Neither could know that Gonzalo de Córdova was to be remembered in history under that title—"The Great Captain."

A silence fell. Happy thoughts filled Pedro's mind. How wrong—how incredibly wrong—he had been about Felipe! And how wonderful it was to learn the truth! Smiling, still silent, they looked at each other. Perhaps it was lantern glow that made their faces so bright. Or perhaps the glow came from within.

Suddenly a new thought occurred to Pedro. "But, Felipe— you said just now that all this had to be kept secret. And— why, you've told me everything!"

Felipe shook his head. "No, not everything. Not quite. There's one thing more." He leaned forward eagerly. "I don't have to keep things secret any longer, Pedro. You see, the peace talks are completed. Boabdil has signed the treaty, and don Gonzalo has just delivered it to Their Highnesses. The word will be announced publicly the first thing tomorrow. The war's over, Pedro—Granada has surrendered!"

The Gates of Granada

It was clear and crisp on that second day of January, 1492. In the vega between Granada and Santa Fe the sunlight rippled on silk and gleamed on steel. The Sovereigns waited there, attended by their entire court, all in rich finery and on splendidly caparisoned mounts. The regiments were drawn up rank on rank, accouterments glinting, standards fluttering.

Pedro's heart beat high with excitement. He blessed the lucky chance which had placed him in a front rank, with an almost unhindered view of the drama taking place. He stood straight and still, with military correctness, but his eager eyes shifted constantly, now right, now left. On the one hand were the Sovereigns and their entourage. On the other, a smaller but equally splendid company was approaching. The rider at its head was superbly mounted and richly dressed. Jewels flashed from his turban and the pendant on his chest; at his waist hung a scimitar with jeweled hilt and sheath.

"Boabdil!" The name rustled through the ranks in loud whispers.

From his point of vantage Pedro could see the Moorish ruler clearly as he rode past. He was young, not over thirty, dark-skinned and black-bearded. He carried himself proudly, head unbowed, but there was infinite sorrow in his face. All in his party displayed similar dignity, riding past with high-held heads, looking neither to right nor left.

Don Ferdinand and doña Isabella rode forward to meet Boabdil. Pedro watched with intent interest as the Moor produced two massive keys—"the keys to the Alhambra," someone in the ranks whispered. With a formal gesture he offered the keys to don Ferdinand, who accepted them with equal formality.

The troops could hear nothing of what was said, but no one missed the eloquent symbolism of the exchange. Boabdil had relinquished not only the Alhambra, but all the power and wealth and glory it signified. Forever lost was his kingdom. Behind him lay Granada, prized city of the Moors, waiting to be claimed by Spanish masters. Every man sensed the drama of this moment. It was not only the end of a war, but of a centuries-long era.

The army watched in silence as Boabdil and his party moved on, their figures slowly diminishing with distance. Presently a stir moved through the ranks, and there were low murmurs of talk.

"Boabdil will still live like a king," Pedro heard someone say. "He has villas and estates in the Alpujarras. His gold and treasures already have been sent on ahead."

"Small comfort he'll find in treasures. An estate isn't a kingdom."

"No. And a villa isn't the Alhambra."

The whispered talk continued, amid a slowly growing tension. A picked regiment had entered Granada earlier to take possession of the Alhambra; now all eyes turned toward the palace-fortress on the hilltop, waiting for the signal that it

was ready for the Sovereigns' entry. The minutes crawled
past. Suspense mounted.

At last, on the Alhambra's highest tower, a group of figures
appeared. Sunlight glinted on metal as a massive silver cross
was raised. Beside it, the standards of Castile and Aragon
were unfurled to float proudly in the light wind.

There was an instant's awed hush. Then a storm of cheering burst out.

*"Granada! Granada for the Sovereigns! Viva doña Isa-
bella! Viva don Ferdinand!"*

The cheering rolled across the vega in a thunderous surge.
But almost at once the exultant clamor faltered, ebbed, died
into silence. All eyes were drawn to the Queen.

Doña Isabella had dismounted and was on her knees, her
eyes upraised, her hands clasped in prayer. Instantly, don
Ferdinand sprang from the saddle and knelt beside her.
Then, with one accord, court and army followed their exam-
ple, and the vega became a sea of kneeling figures, pouring out
fervent thanks to God. Hearts beat high, eyes misted as they
looked at the silver symbol on the tower, the Christian Cross
shining where the Moslem Crescent had reigned for over
seven centuries.

There was no more cheering. A solemn hush held the multitude as the Sovereigns remounted and turned their horses
toward Granada. As they rode slowly past the spot where
Pedro was stationed he caught a clear view of doña Isabella's
face. It was radiant. Tears of joy shone in her eyes as she
gazed toward the cross and the banners on the tower.

Pedro watched her until she was past. Then his glance
swept quickly over the retinue which followed, scarcely notic-

ing the pomp and pageantry of the spectacle. Eagerly his eyes searched the procession, and fixed on a rider near the rear. Simply dressed, the man cut a sober figure amid so much magnificence—and fittingly so, Pedro thought. Captain Columbus needed no glittering trappings to lend him nobility.

The man's expression held that same rapt quality which had lighted doña Isabella's face. How alike they were, the Genoese mariner and the Castilian Queen! Worlds apart in birth and station, yet how strangely interlinked were their lives! She had battled for a kingdom. He had battled for a dream. And Granada's surrender spelt victory for both.

Columbus seemed unaware of his surroundings. His gaze was fixed straight ahead, but Pedro knew he was not looking at Granada. It was a far horizon he saw, an unknown sea—beckoning, challenging, promising. Pedro caught the fire of that same vision. He watched Columbus ride past, watched his receding figure move on toward the gates of Granada, so long forbiddingly closed, now at last swung wide.

A strange thought came to Pedro—a thought so overwhelming that he could only grasp it vaguely. That wide-flung portal opened not only upon a fabulous city, but upon a future that was bright with promise for all men.

It was a gateway to a new Spain, a new era, a New World.

By the same author

THE ANGRY EARTH

For hundreds of years the Spaniards had fought to drive the Moors out of Spain, and now in the year 1491 the army laid siege to Granada, the last remaining Moorish stronghold. In that army was fifteen-year-old Pedro Tegero, an orphan who had been brought up from infancy by the friars of Santa Maria de la Rábida. Pedro wanted to be a sailor, but for a very special reason he had chosen to be a soldier instead.

At the monastery he had met a remarkable man who had a fantastic dream of sailing westward across the vast ocean to reach the Indies. Pedro believed passionately that Captain Columbus could do this and the Captain had promised him a place as cabin boy if ever a sponsor could be found who was willing to provide ships. Queen Isabella, too, believed in the dream, and Pedro was hopeful that she would soon agree to finance the enterprise. He did not want to be far away on a ship in the Mediterranean when this happened!

Through all the crowding events of the siege —a battle with the Moors, the burning of the Spanish camp, the gallant building of the city of Santa Fe—Pedro's thoughts turned continuously to his hero, and to the great day when the Moors would surrender and the Queen would commit her support to the noble venture for the glory of Spain.

Filled with scenes of drama and pageantry, and peopled with a colorful cast of characters, this is a book that gives the reader an exhilarating sense of being involved in the unfolding of history.

Granada,
Surrender!

About the author

CARL KIDWELL was born and grew up in Washington, Indiana. He worked at various jobs before joining the Navy, where he became a radio operator. He had always liked to draw and did a lot of sketching aboard ship in his free time. When the war was over, he became a professional artist. His illustrations appeared in Western and adventure magazines, and several books. Eventually he began to write as well.

An earlier book, *The Angry Earth,* was the result of a visit to Mexico which led him to delve into that country's archaeological history. *Granada, Surrender!,* too, grew out of his interest in searching out little-known incidents in history.